MIKE RESNICK

Kilimanjaro:
A Fable of Utopia

KILIMANJARO:
A FABLE OF UTOPIA

MIKE RESNICK

SUBTERRANEAN PRESS 2008

First Edition

ISBN
978-1-59606-199-6

Subterranean Press
PO Box 190106
Burton, MI 48519

www.subterraneanpress.com

For Carol, as always,

and for

Janis Ian, the kid sister I never had
&
Lesley Ainge, the granddaughter I never had

PROLOGUE (2234 A.D.)

THE most impressive sight in Africa is the snow-capped peak of mighty Kilimanjaro, the tallest mountain on the continent. The greatest elephant that ever lived was killed on Kilimanjaro's southern slopes, and my people believed that En-kai, our god, dwells at the summit. On a clear day it can be seen from more than seventy miles away. There was a time when the mountain was home to more than a million animals, as well as to the Maasai people. Elephants, rhinos, and buffalo rubbed shoulders beneath the acacia trees, while lions and leopards lay in wait for unsuspecting antelope by the water holes. Areas where the slopes flattened out were covered by our *manyattas*.

But that was long ago.

There are no more animals on the mountain, and precious few people. Today the Maasai live on another Kilimanjaro, and it is this Kilimanjaro that I have been tasked to tell you about.

It was in the year 2122 A.D. that the Eutopian worlds were terraformed in orbit around Earth, and the Eutopian Council allowed seventy-three groups, each striving to create their own cultural Utopia, to charter the seventy-three worlds. Not all of the worlds fared as well as they had hoped. The Communist world went bankrupt; a Moslem world erupted into a brutal civil war; a fundamentalist Christian world waited for God to provide rather than tilling their fields and planting their crops and did not ask for help until most of them had starved to death. Other worlds had other problems. Some overcame them and flourished; some were overwhelmed and eventually abandoned.

But there was one world that interested my people above all others, and that was Kirinyaga, the only Eutopian world settled by an African tribe—the Kikuyu. And since the Maasai have shared Kenya with the Kikuyu for millennia, we studied every aspect of the planetoid and its society, every triumph and every failure, determined to learn from their mistakes.

In the early days, under the leadership of a man named Koriba, there were far more failures than triumphs. Indeed, it was only after Koriba returned to Kenya that Kirinyaga began to function cohesively...and yet, somewhere along the way, they had forgotten the purpose of the Eutopian worlds, which was to create a true cultural Utopia. Kirinyaga is now 112 years old and still thriving, but in truth it is thriving as an extension of Kenya, not as an independent world that is correcting all the inequities of Kenyan, or even Kikuyu, society.

My people were finally awarded a Eutopian world in 2234 A.D., after many years, even decades, of lobbying. Since the Kikuyu had named their world for the mountain upon which their god dwelt, we decided to do the same—and no one can deny that Kilimanjaro is the more imposing mountain of the two, just as En-kai was thought to be a more powerful god than the Kikuyu's Ngai.

Upon receiving our charter, we worked closely with the terraformers, deciding upon the contours and make-up the landscape, which animals and birds to clone, which vegetation would cover the ground. We also decided, as I mentioned, that before we emigrated to Kilimanjaro we would make a thorough study of Kirinyaga's history so we could avoid all of the mistakes that they had made.

Understanding and pinpointing those mistakes is part of my job. I am David ole Saitoti, which means "David, son of Saitoti", and I am, by profession, an historian. I was one of a half dozen assigned to study all aspects of Kirinyaga, and since I'm the only one who chose to emigrate to Kilimanjaro, I have been entrusted with the task of recording Kilimanjaro's history.

Merely inhabiting an empty world is a monumental chore. Turning that world into a Maasai Utopia is an even greater one. I do not expect to be able to write a daily diary, but I will codify the more important episodes in our early history as time allows.

I don't yet know exactly what shape our Utopia will take, but with all the examples we have to learn from, and especially from Kirinyaga, I know this much:

This time we will do it right.

1 Sunrise on Kilimanjaro (2234 A.D.)

THE Kikuyu were slaves to their tradition, and this was a mistake we were determined to avoid. One size doesn't fit all, and neither does one way of life.

The Maasai were among the last people on Earth to break with tradition, and for those who still chose to live the traditional pastoral lifestyle, we arranged for fully half of Kilimanjaro to be open grazing land.

Before the coming of the Europeans, almost every African tribe used cattle as currency. A bride would cost so many cattle, a chief would penalize a wrongdoer so many cattle, and so on. For the Maasai the cattle were even more important, for most of us, and especially our *elmoran*—our young warriors—lived on a mixture of the blood and milk. When our religious ceremonies required it we would sacrifice a steer or a cow and cook and eat it, but their primary purpose was to serve as currency and to provide blood and milk.

The Westernized Maasai cast aside their red blankets and began wearing slacks, shirts, dresses, and suits. They rid their heads of their red ocher paints, they traded their cattle for cash and their spears for briefcases. And yet they were Maasai too, and had to be accommodated.

So we had *manyattas* for the traditionalists, and cities for the rest of us. There were some farms as well, for while many Maasai chose to exist solely on the milk, blood and meat of their cattle, others had grown used to a Western diet.

There are five cities on our world. I have read much speculation concerning that number: some feel five is a mystic number to the Maasai, some say we had wanted to build more cities but were denied funding, and I have even read one so-called scholar who opined that we could count no higher than the five fingers on our hand. (Evidently he never realized that Maasai are born with two hands—or perhaps he had only one, and assumed that everyone else did also.)

Anyway, the truth is much simpler than the speculations: the Maasai are comprised of five clans—the *ilmakesen, il-laiser, il-molelian, il-taarrosero,* and *il-ikumai*, and we built a city for each of them, though of course no one is restricted to the city of his clan.

Immigration is encouraged, for we have a world to fill. Each potential new citizen is given an orientation course, for we don't want anyone deciding once they arrive that this is not the Utopia they had hoped for. Part of that indoctrination is a holo of all aspects of life on Kilimanjaro, those that exist and those that are anticipated, so there will be no surprises. Another part is a documentary holo— a re-creation, actually, since nothing Western was allowed there, including cameras—of the first two decades of Kirinyaga's history, so they can see how the best of intentions can go wrong, and hopefully understand that when certain laws and rules are made and enforced it isn't done in an idealistic vacuum, but because we have learned from others' mistakes.

We are so sure that Kilimanjaro will prove to be the one world that actually fulfills its Utopian promise, that we have decided we need a policy to determine who will receive favored status for immigration once we have filled our empty plains and cities. In fact, this is the first major decision the Council of Elders will have to make.

The Eutopian Council, which gave us our charter, gently hinted that they would like to see a democracy develop on Kilimanjaro, and perhaps someday it will, but only if it evolves out of the Maasai tradition, and that tradition is to bring all disputes to the elders of the tribe. Local problems are dealt with by local Councils, but since the problem of immigration concerns the entire world, in this case the Council is composed of one Elder from each of the five cities, and two from the land of the *manyattas*.

The first question was: who may immigrate to Kilimanjaro once we have reached fifty percent of our capacity?

The answer was simple: this is a Maasai world, so at that point only Maasai may immigrate.

The next question was more difficult: who is a Maasai?

Those who had always tended their cattle and lived in their huts on their *manyattas* are traditional Maasai, but these days, in the 23rd century of the Christian era, they comprise no more than twenty percent of our population. Most of the Maasai have moved to the great cities such as Nairobi and Dar Es Salaam, Naivasha and Dodoma, and have interbred—is that the right word? It is the most accurate, though I think the Council prefers "intermarried"—with members of other races: the Kikuyu, the Luo, the Nandi, the Zanake, and more.

The Council debated this for four days, and decided that anyone with one-half Maasai blood is a Maasai.

That was when we began to see that *no* problem is that easily solved in Utopia.

Joshua ole Saibull, who had been an attorney back on Earth, and whose mother was Indian, argued that this was a distinction that would disenfranchise future generations.

When asked how, this is what he replied:

"I myself am half Maasai. My wife's father was a Rendille, and her mother a Maasai. So it is clear that we are each half Maasai, and this will also be true of our children."

"But," he continued, "if at any time in the past thousand years any of my forefathers had a child by a woman who was not Maasai—and don't forget that we used to raid the Kikuyu and other tribes and carry off their women—then a DNA test will show that I am less than half Maasai, possibly forty-nine percent, possibly forty-five percent, but definitely less than half. I am here, my wife is here, and I fully understand that no one is denying us the right to be citizens of Kilimanjaro. But my children and my grandchildren will also test out at less than fifty percent Maasai, and the day may come when Kilimanjaro has more people than it can handle. At that point will you force my children to leave the planet?"

The Council of Elders replied that of course they would not.

"Even if my children are only forty percent Maasai?" persisted Joshua.

Even so, they assured him.

"That is very considerate of you," said Joshua, as if he were speaking to a jury, and in a way he was. "Now, what if a potential immigrant is forty-eight percent Maasai? Will you deny him the right to live on a Maasai world, while my forty-percent-Maasai children are allowed to stay?"

The Council of Elders was still considering the ramifications of that argument when another one was presented to them.

"My name," said the supplicant, "is Kella Jimo, and prior to coming to Kilimanjaro I lived in Kenya's Northern Frontier District until a long drought killed my cattle and dried up my wells." He waited until the sudden whispering and buzzing had stopped. "Yes, I am a Samburu. And yet I claim I have every bit as much right to be here as any of you, for once the Samburu and the Maasai were a single tribe. We both spoke the language of Maa, we both worshipped En-kai, we both shared the same blood. If you take the DNA of any Samburu and trace it back, you will find we are pure Maasai, certainly moreso than Joshua ole Saibull or any others who have lived in the cities of Kenya and Tanzania and intermarried with other tribes. I therefore insist that by your own ruling the Samburu have as much right to Kilimanjaro as the Maasai."

They are still studying *that* one, too.

However, while one might view these as time bombs that will explode many decades in the future, they are meaningless right now. We have a world to fill and more immediate problems to confront.

One of our most pressing problems is the economy. The city dwellers use cash and credit; the pastoralists use cattle. The Council of Elders must fix the price of a single cow if there is ever to be any commerce between the two sets of citizens. The pastoralists will not save or invest money; the city dwellers have no place for cattle even if they were willing to keep them. Since we will not force either side to live in a way that is repugnant to them, we have to find a way to accommodate both sides.

An historian's job is not only to codify history but to learn from it, and what I have learned is that whatever price the Council of Elders sets, the city dwellers will claim that it is too high and the pastoralists will claim that it is too low.

And yet, when the accusations are over, the Council *will* set a price, both sides *will* agree to it since there is no higher authority to appeal to, and that will be the end of another potential stumbling block on the road to our Utopia.

Then there is the matter of language. When the Samburu said that his people and ours both spoke Maa, he was correct insofar as he went. But more than ninety-five percent of the Maasai speak Swahili, which is the *lingua franca* among the peoples of East Africa, and ninety percent speak English, which has occasionally been the official language of Kenya and is still the language of business, commerce, and diplomacy.

What language are we to use? If we remain purists and speak only Maa, then no one offworld will understand us. If we speak English, we will be using the language of our former enemies. And if we use Swahili, we will be using neither our own tongue nor the language of the Eutopian Council and much of Earth itself. It is another problem we had not foreseen, but which we will soon have to solve. My guess is that since all three tongues are known to most of the people we will resolve the problem by ignoring it. If you speak a language that the party you are addressing understands, it makes no difference to the two of you what that language is; and if he does not understand it, common sense dictates that the two of you will experiment with other languages until you come to one you both comprehend.

I find this an exciting time. These are merely growing pains, and I suspect we will have less of them than any of the other Eutopian worlds. One of my functions is to preserve our history, but an equally important one is to help our people learn from the failed histories of the other worlds.

One of the things I've learned is that Kirinyaga and many of the other worlds relied too heavily on the assumed wisdom of a single man, such as Koriba. This will not happen on Kilimanjaro. Every citizen has something to offer, and it would be foolhardy of our leaders not to avail themselves of it:

For example, the Maasai have produced some of East Africa's finest medical doctors, and some of them have chosen to emigrate to Kilimanjaro, where each of the five cities has an up-to-date hospital.

Kirinyaga's *mundumugu* may have been expected to cure every illness, but here the patient will see a trained specialist.

We have lived in harmony with Nature for untold centuries, so we created two large game parks, filled with the clones of long-extinct hippos, rhinos, plains game, and just the right ratio of predators so that they neither multiply beyond the parks' ability to feed them or fail to produce enough numbers to replace those who have fallen prey to the lions, leopards and hyenas. The parks are surrounded by a force field so that neither the herbivores nor the predators can ever get out to annoy or threaten the nearby pastoralists.

Perhaps the most important thing we have done to improve the peoples' lives is the near-total eradication of flies. The huts of the pastoralists are made of cattle dung, and the dung is also spread throughout the *manyattas*. This attracted myriad flies, which often carried disease. They were omnipresent and annoying, they tended to light on the eyes, and they blinded more than one Maasai child. Our chemists went to work, and now we have a planet without a single fly.

Many have moved here already, and in two more days the last of the cities, the lakes and rivers, the grazing fields, and the *manyattas* will be complete. There is even a small church with a steeple out on the pastoralists' lands, for those who have converted to Christianity. Just 48 hours from now our Utopia will be, as the Maintenance crew that built it says, open for business.

I can hardly wait.

2 MORNING ON KILIMANJARO (2235 A.D.)

WE have had so many applicants for citizenship that I've revised my opinion downward: we will be screening potential immigrants for the "purity" of their blood in less than ten years.

The cities are already half full. It is more difficult to tell with the *manyattas*, since all the grazing land is available and the pastoralists have spread their herds out to cover it. I hope we do not have any problems getting them to share it as more newcomers arrive.

I think that, by and large, our first eight months have gone smoothly. There have been a few disputes over territory, but since we momentarily have an abundance of territory they were quickly settled. There were, as I foresaw, endless complaints about the exchange rate that was finally set for cattle, but eventually both sides accepted the Council's ruling.

One of the unforeseen problems was the value of the shilling itself. It was decided that since shillings were the currency in Kenya and Tanzania, they would also be the currency here on Kilimanjaro, and this is where we ran into difficulties. The Kenya shilling is worth more than the Tanzania shilling, so when the price of a cow was set at seven hundred shillings, the pastoralists refused to accept Tanzania shillings and insisted they be paid only in Kenya shillings.

It was then decided that a new world required a new currency, and so we created the Kilimanjaro shilling. This presented another problem, for we were inexperienced in such matters. You cannot simply print shillings, or they are worth no more than the paper they are printed on. They must be pegged to something: gold, silver, or some other currency.

We decided to peg ours to the Kenya shilling, since it was the currency with which we were most familiar. Any immigrant could change his Kenya shillings for Kilimanjaro shillings at the posted rate. It seemed simple enough.

But then Kenya went into a recession, and suddenly the Kenya shilling, which was pegged to the British pound, was worth about half what it had been when we had pegged our shilling to it. It was only after some of our city dwellers paid visits to their families back in Kenya, and returned with huge amounts of devalued Kenya shillings, that we had to devalue our currency, and suddenly our own economy was in a deeper recession than Kenya's.

We then announced that the rate of exchange between cattle and shillings would change daily. The pastoralists were certain that this was a way of defrauding them, and the city dwellers objected to the value of our currency depending on the financial actions of the country we had left behind.

Eventually this was solved for the simple reason that we could not survive with only a barter economy when the city dwellers had nothing to offer the pastoralists, and the pastoralists had only cattle to offer the city dwellers.

It was painful, and there were some awkward dislocations, but we were fast learners, and even as I write these words the economy is slowly recovering.

Which is just as well, because other minor problems continue to surface. Some were predictable, and we had prepared for them. Some were completely unforeseen, and required innovative solutions.

Like "ole".

As I mentioned in a previous entry, "ole" means "son of". Some typical Maasai names are my own David ole Saitoti (David, son of Saitoti), our leading lawyer Joshua ole Saibull (Joshua, son of Saibull), and so on.

Now let me give you the names of my sister, Joshua's wife, and my neighbor's wife: Esiankiki, Malaika, and Ledama.

Do you see the difference?

Ledama did, and so she took her complaint to the Council of Elders.

"Women were treated as second-class citizens for centuries when we still lived in Africa," she began. "We did almost all the physical labor, while our men protected the herds from the lions and leopards, even long after there were no longer any lions and leopards to protect them from. It wasn't until we moved to Nairobi and Mombasa and the other cities that we began asserting ourselves and were finally treated as equals."

"You are still treated as equals," said Robert ole Meeli, who spoke for the Council. "What is your complaint?"

"We are *not* treated as equals," insisted Ledama.

"In what way?" asked Robert. "No job is closed to you, every job pays the same amount no matter who is working at it, no establishment refuses you entry. So I repeat: what is your complaint?"

"There is an inequity in names," said Ledama.

Robert looked confused. "An inequity in *names*?"

"You are Robert son of Meeli," she said. "I am merely Ledama."

"Would you rather be known as Ledama ole Koyati?" he asked, and the other Elders chuckled.

"I am not the son of anyone," said Ledama. "But why can't I be Ledama daughter of Koyati?"

"It would be a break with a thousand-year tradition," explained Robert.

"Then you admit that even after a thousand years you do not think of us as equals," said Ledama. "Is Kilimanjaro to be a Utopia only for men?"

The Council conferred for less than half an hour, one of its briefer meetings, and declared that from that day forward she could be Ledama daughter of Koyati. And that solved the problem.

For twenty-four hours.

Because the next day Ashina, the daughter of Lemasolai, brought her complaint to the Elders.

"Why must I be known as the daughter of Lemasolai?" she demanded.

"Isn't he your father?" asked Robert ole Meeli.

"Yes."

"Then it's settled," he said.

"It is *not* settled," she insisted. "Didn't you just reaffirm yesterday that the sexes are equal on Kilimanjaro?"

"Yes," said Robert, frowning and trying to figure out where this was leading.

"My mother was Kibibi," continued Ashina. "What makes my father more important than my mother?"

"We have never said that he was," answered Robert.

"Then my name should Ashina daughter of Kibibi."

This time it took the Council only ten minutes to agree.

"This subject is now closed," pronounced Robert ole Meeli. "If someone shows up tomorrow demanding to be known as the son or daughter of both parents, I will personally take him to the game park and throw him—"

"Or *her*," interjected Ashina.

"Or her," he continued, "to the lions."

It was an embarrassing two days, even humiliating if you were Robert ole Meeli, but at the end of it women knew beyond any doubt that they were equal citizens of Kilimanjaro.

Until the following week, when Ledama stood before the Council of Elders again, demanding to know why no women were on the Council.

This was a greater break with tradition than anything that had gone before, but there was always that telling argument: is Kilimanjaro a Utopia for all its citizens, or only half of them?

Finally the Council agreed to increase its number from seven to thirteen, and the six new members would be women, one from each of the five cities and one from the *manyattas*.

This was *almost* equal, Ledama pointed out, but it still left one more man than woman on the ruling body.

There *must* be an odd number on the Council so that there will be no deadlocks, answered Robert.

Then make the extra member a woman, said Ledama.

This would not be fair to the men, came the answer.

The men have been unfair to us for centuries, argued Ledama. View this as reparation.

I am not responsible for what my great-great-great-grandfathers may have done, said Robert, and I will not make reparation for their sins.

Ledama argued, but the Council remained adamant. The next week there were thirteen members of the Council of Elders, seven men and six women.

And the day after that, Robert ole Meeli's wife left him and went to live among the pastoralists.

3 Mid-Morning on Kilimanjaro (2236 A.D.)

I was sitting in my office, going over some notes I had entered in my computer, when there was a knock at the door. I have no secretary or receptionist, so I just called out "Come in!"

The door remained closed, so I got up, walked across the office, opened it, and found myself facing a tall thin boy of twelve or thirteen. He was clearly from a pastoralist family, for he wore the traditional red blanket and carried a spear. He was barefoot, his hair was carefully braided, and he looked like he needed another twenty pounds on his body.

"Hello," I said in English. "Didn't you hear me?"

"You are David ole Saitoti?" he responded in Maa, ignoring my question.

"I am," I said, switching to Maa. "Won't you come in?"

He looked carefully around my office as if expecting to find demons awaiting him, which was obviously why he hadn't entered when I first called out. When he found no hidden monsters he finally nodded his head and entered, taking up the traditional herders' position, with one leg on the floor, the other bent with the foot pressed against his shin, leaning on his spear.

"Please sit down," I said, walking behind my desk and sitting in my own chair, which hovered a few inches above the ground and changed its shape to firmly encircle me.

"I do not trust chairs that float in the air," he said. "I will sit only on a three-legged stool, such as we have in my parents' *manyata*."

"Then you shall have to remain standing," I said. "What is your name?"

"Mawenzi ole Porola," he replied.

It was very rare to find a Maasai who did not have a Western name, and I must have looked my surprise.

"My father, who named me, did not forget our traditions," said Mawenzi with a note of pride. "I hope you have not forgotten them either, or my journey here was wasted." He paused. "It was very hard to find my way among the streets and buildings of the city."

"Why have you come all this way to see me?" I asked.

"You are the historian, are you not?"

"Yes."

"Then you are the man I must see."

"If you're having problems in one of your classes…" I began.

"I do not take classes," he said haughtily. "I am a true Maasai."

"Almost everyone on Kilimanjaro is a true Maasai," I replied. "That doesn't mean they have to remain ignorant."

"I do not seek lectures from you, only answers."

"I can't promise to give you the one without the other," I said, turning back to my computer. "Perhaps you can find what you need elsewhere."

"*No!*" he all-but-shouted.

I stared at him but said nothing.

"I need *you!*" he insisted.

"You cannot always have what you want, let alone what you need," I replied. "I will not be spoken to in such a manner."

He was silent for a moment, obviously battling within himself. Finally his whole body seemed to relax.

"I apologize for my arrogance," he said.

"You see?" I said with a smile. "Even a Maasai can apologize, and the world doesn't come to an end."

"You are a very strange Maasai," said Mawenzi.

"And you are a very troubled one," I said. "Would you like to tell me about it?"

He nodded. "My father—my *true* father—is dead."

"I'm sorry."

"It was a long time ago," he said distractedly. "And my mother has wed again."

"That is good," I said.

"That is the problem," replied Mawenzi.

"You don't like your new father?"

"He is a good man. He provides for us, he is never too stern, he cares for my two sisters and myself as if we were his own children."

"Now that he has married your mother, you *are* his children," I pointed out.

"He has never beat us," continued Mawenzi. "We have never gone hungry, our cattle are healthy and fertile, and he is a respected elder." He paused. "There can be no doubt of it: he is a good man."

"I take it that he is also somehow connected with your problem?" I asked.

He nodded. "Yes. Even though he is a good man, I must pit you against him, and you must triumph."

I did a double-take at that. "You're not seriously suggesting that I fight your new father?"

"No. He would kill you very easily."

"Then perhaps you'd better tell me exactly what your problem is, and what you expect me to do about it."

"I am fourteen years old," said Mawenzi. "Next month I was to be circumcised in the ceremony that will turn me from a boy into a man. My father chooses to live in the old way, herding his cattle, but he has been to school in Kenya, and he reads books."

"And he doesn't want you circumcised?" I said.

"He calls it barbaric, and refuses to allow it." Suddenly the arrogance was gone, and it was all Mawenzi could do to hold back his tears. "If I am not circumcised with the rest of my age group, I can never take a wife or have my own *manyatta*. All I ask is not to be different from my peers. I do not wish to move to the city, or learn the secrets of your computers. I do not wish to fly high above the ground in the airplanes that pass overhead. I want only to be a man, and be accorded a man's rights. Is that so much to ask?"

"No, it isn't," I answered.

"You are an historian," he continued. "You can speak to my new father, can tell him that this is our tradition, that it has always been done this way. He himself was circumcised as a boy, or he could never have married my mother, or cut off his braids and painted his head with red ocher. Why should he deny me what he himself possesses?"

I couldn't help but admire young Mawenzi's intelligence. He knew he needed help to convince his father to let him undergo the ritual, but he also knew that none of the neighboring elders who had to work with his father would be likely to argue with him over this, so he used his brain and came up with the one person who could best explain the sanctity of Maasai traditions—an historian.

But while I admired Mawenzi's intellect I also resented it, because up to this moment I had been a student and a chronicler of life on Kilimanjaro, and now he wanted me to become an active participant.

My first thought was that his stepfather would run me through with his spear for having the temerity to interfere in his family's problems. But then I thought of Mawenzi, who would of course grow up to be a man, but would never be convinced that he had reached manhood until he had been circumcised.

I was still considering my reaction when Mawenzi spoke up.

"You have been silent for a long time," he said. "Is something wrong?"

"No," I said. "I'm thinking."

"Will explain to my father why I must be circumcised?"

"You came all this way and sought me out in a city that is very strange and frightening to you," I began.

"It is strange," he agreed. "But I am a Maasai. Nothing frightens me."

"Fine," I said. "You have found me and asked for my help. You will find it hard to believe, but no one has ever asked for my help before, and I was very content with that. But if you're not afraid to come here, what kind of Maasai would I be if I were afraid to help you?"

He tried to hide his relief, but didn't quite manage.

"Tonight you'll sleep in my apartment," I said, "and tomorrow we'll go to your *manyatta* and see your father."

He looked underfed—*all* the pastoralists looked underfed—and I decided he needed a meal. I knew better than to take him to a restaurant, so I took him to my apartment and fixed him a beef sandwich. He stared at it suspiciously—he had never seen sliced bread before—but finally he took a bite, and then another, and he wolfed it down so fast that I made him another, which he ate almost as quickly. I offered him a glass of milk, which he refused because it had no blood in it. Then I made him a dish of ice cream. I had some strawberry syrup, and I poured some of it onto the ice cream. It looked just enough like blood that he was willing to try it, and I could tell by his face that he might never miss the city but he would miss ice cream every day for the rest of his life.

I brought him to my guest room and showed him the bed, then went to my own room. When I woke up the next morning, I saw that he had pulled the mattress onto the floor and had slept on it that way.

Mawenzi had ice cream for breakfast, and then I got my car out of the garage. He had seen cars almost every day, but he had never ridden in one. Before long he was hanging so far out of the window, looking at every passing sight, that I was afraid he might fall out if I hit a bump.

Finally we arrived at his *manyatta*, a series of mud-and-dung huts clustered together, surrounded by a fence made from the branches of thorn trees. The fence served no purpose—historically all the family's cattle would be enclosed at night to protect them from predators, but there *were* no predators any longer—but Mawenzi's family, like most of the pastoralists, still honored the tradition. All of Mawenzi's siblings—there were five of them, two by his blood father, three by his adopted father—came up, wide-eyed and curious, to see the car. A minute later a grown man wearing a t-shirt and shorts walked up, and I knew this must be Mawenzi's stepfather.

"Has Mawenzi gotten in trouble?" he asked in English.

"No," I replied.

"Good. I was worried when I saw your car. Clearly you're from the city. What was he doing there?"

"He sought me out to ask my advice," I said carefully. Since we were speaking English, I extended my hand. "I'm David ole Saitoti."

"I am Samuel," he replied.

"Just Samuel?"

"Samuel is enough. What particular advice has Mawenzi sought?"

"He needed my expertise as an historian," I said.

He nodded his head. "I thought as much. Let's walk and talk. There's no need to discuss this in front of my children."

He began walking off toward his cattle, and I joined him.

"It's about the circumcision ceremony, isn't it?" said Samuel.

"Yes, it is," I answered.

"And he has told you that I'm a cruel, unfeeling man and a false Maasai?"

"No, Samuel," I said. "He has the utmost respect for you."

"Really?" he said. "That's surprising. I know how much this means to him."

"Then why not let him be circumcised?" I asked.

"I have my reasons."

"Perhaps you'd care to share them with me," I suggested.

"You're an historian," he replied. "You've come here at Mawenzi's request, to argue his case. You're going to tell me that this has been the Maasai's ritual passage to manhood for millennia, and that I'm shaming him by not permitting it."

"Do you care for him?" I asked.

"I love him as if he were my own blood son," said Samuel.

"Then why are you denying him his passage to adulthood?"

"It's a brutal, barbaric custom!" snapped Samuel.

"Yet you yourself were circumcised," I pointed out.

"Yes, I was."

"And it did you no harm."

"None."

"Then why—?"

He seemed to consider his answer for a long moment. Then he stopped walking and turned to me. "Mawenzi's mother is not my first wife," he said. "My first wife died—but before she died, I had a son. He was very much like Mawenzi: bold, courageous, intelligent. And like Mawenzi, he took great pride in being a Maasai and in honoring our traditions."

"Including circumcision?" I asked.

"Including circumcision," said Samuel.

"He should be a young man now," I said, wondering where this was leading. "Does he live on Kilimanjaro?"

"He's dead," said Samuel, and I could see the emotional pain in his face. "He died from an infection caused by the circumcision ceremony. It was on that day that I rid myself of all names except Samuel, I cast aside my red blanket, I began to grow my hair, and I swore that no child of mine would ever be circumcised again."

"I see," I said.

"It is a brutal custom," he continued. "We have hospitals that insist on sterile instruments, on disposable gloves for surgeons and nurses, on antiseptic cleansers for everything within the building. And yet when I was circumcised I stood knee-deep in a polluted stream, and was cut by a knife that had cut every member of my circumcision group, that still bore their blood. I knew that no Maasai is supposed to show pain, so I stood there like a statue, despite the agony I felt, unaware of the possible effects of the ceremony. I was proud of myself, and years later I was equally proud to have my son undergo the same ritual. When he became ill I took him to the *laiboni,* and only when the *laiboni* could not cure him did I take him to the hospital in the city, where they told me they could not save him, that we had waited too long. On that day I discarded my red blanket, threw away my spear, and allowed my hair to grow long again." A look of fierce defiance spread across his features. "I will not lose another son to this madness!"

"I see," I said. The *laiboni* is the witch doctor.

"Is that so cruel?" he demanded.

"It's not cruel at all," I said. "But it can have cruel consequences. Mawenzi will not be allowed to take a wife, or to start his own *manyatta.*"

"Only if he remains out here," he said, indicating the savannah with a sweeping gesture. "This won't hamper him in the city."

"But he wants to live a traditional life as a pastoralist," I pointed out, "and this will be denied him."

"If what happened to my son happens to him, *all* life will be denied him," replied Samuel firmly.

"There must be a compromise," I said.

"There's no solution that will please both sides," said Samuel.

"That's possible," I said. "But I promised Mawenzi I would try, and I'm going to keep my word to him."

He walked off to tend to his cattle, and I remained where I was, analyzing the situation. It did indeed seem insoluble, because each side had a strong moral argument: Samuel did not want Mawenzi endangered, which was reasonable and displayed a father's love and concern; and Mawenzi wanted his birthright, his passage to adulthood, which was equally reasonable.

Slowly it dawned on me that if the problem were to be considered in that light, it would require an ethicist to solve it, because it was clearly an ethical dilemma.

But I am not an ethicist. I am an historian, and I knew that if I were to find a satisfactory solution, it would be because I used my special knowledge. And when I realized that was the approach I must take, I began to see how the problem could be resolved.

Finally I walked back to Mawenzi's hut. He was there, trying not to appear too hopeful or too surly. I told him to have one of his siblings go out into the fields and bring Samuel back to the hut. When he arrived, I had both of them sit on their low three-legged stools, while I stood across the hut, facing them.

"You have asked for my help," I said to Mawenzi. "And you," I said to Samuel, "haven't denied me the right to try to help."

"That's true," said Samuel.

"I'm an historian," I continued, "so it is to history that I look for guidance. Now, there is almost no Maasai history before the 18th century A.D., some five centuries ago—but that doesn't mean that all history began then. The Chinese and Egyptians have histories that go back thousands of years, and more to the point, so do the Jews. And the Jews were circumcising their male children millennia before there *was* a Maasai tribe."

"Do they still?" asked Mawenzi.

"They do," I said. "But they don't do it in streams or rivers, and they don't do it with unsterilized instruments. In almost every case they do it in hospitals under conditions that guarantee no one will ever suffer or become ill from the process. Many Christians are also circumcised in hospitals."

I turned to Samuel. "If Mawenzi is circumcised in the hospital, will you have any objection?"

"No," he said.

"Mawenzi," I said, "if you are circumcised alone, not by a *laiboni* but by a doctor, will this satisfy you?"

"Can't the doctor come and circumcise all of us in the traditional way?" he asked.

I shook my head. "No doctor will agree to that, because it could cause infection and disease."

Mawenzi seemed lost in thought for a moment. Then he looked up. "I will agree to it, as long as it is known in the *manyattas* that I have been circumcised."

"It will be," promised Samuel.

The next morning Mawenzi became the first Maasai to be circumcised under sterile conditions by a medical doctor.

And then something strange happened. Suddenly most of the young men asked to be circumcised in the same way, for they could see no reason for suffering pain if they didn't have to. They were proud young men, and none would have volunteered to be the first, but once Mawenzi did it, they had no problem following suit.

It was when some of the girls asked to be circumcised in the hospital that the doctors categorically refused, claiming that it served no medical purpose and was a cruel and unnatural surgery that was in fact against Nature's intentions. The girls are still circumcised in the old way—but a few have refused, and I think next year even more will refuse. We can't win every battle, but if we persist, eventually we can win the war.

All that happened three months ago. There has yet to be a sign of infection, all because of one boy who insisted on honoring a tradition that his father opposed, and one historian who found the solution not among the Maasai but rather with a much older tribe.

4 Noon on Kilimanjaro (2237 A.D.)

I had just come back from a drive through the game park, which I always find relaxing. For centuries the Maasai had lived in harmony with the land, had shared that land with the creatures of the African wilderness, and then one day, seemingly overnight, there were no such creatures left. The great cats, the pachyderms, all the herbivores and carnivores, were gone. Poaching had reduced their numbers, of course, but it was habitat destruction that was the true cause of their extinction. Animals can come back from poaching, or from disease, or from drought—but once humanity has taken over their habitat, there is no place for them to come back *to*. So it was very pleasant, especially for an historian who knew the way we used to live, to be able to sit in my car by a water hole, watching the impalas and zebras and elands and buffalo come down to drink.

When I returned to my office, I found my friend Joshua ole Saibull, the lawyer, pacing restlessly back and forth in the foyer of the building.

"Hello, David," he said in English when he saw me. "Where the hell were you?"

"At the game park," I replied.

"Again?" he said with an amused laugh. "Are you an historian or a naturalist?"

"I'm just a person who finds it relaxing to watch wildlife," I said. "I assume you're here to see me?"

"Why else would I come to a cramped little building filled with academics?"

"Well, come into my office and tell me what I can do for you."

"For me, nothing," he said as I walked down the corridor, stopped by my door, and uttered the combination that unlocked it. He followed me as I walked into the interior of the cluttered room. "For William Blumlein, everything."

"Who is William Blumlein?" I asked as he sat down on the same chair that Mawenzi had refused a year ago.

"You're spending too much of your time dwelling in the past," said Joshua.

"That's my job."

"This is a man that historians will be studying and praising a century from now."

"Enlighten me," I said, finally sitting down behind my desk.

"William Blumlein is one of the leading sociologists on Earth," said Joshua.

"William Blumlein," I repeated. "Is he white?"

"Yes," he said.

"I assumed as much from his name," I said. "Well, tell me about him."

"He wants to live here," said Joshua. "He's spent the past decade studying the Maasai in Kenya and Tanzania, and now he wants to immigrate to Kilimanjaro and spend the rest of his life right here, researching us."

"Why?" I asked.

"Why do you study our history?" shot back Joshua. "He's fascinated by the Maasai. The only difference is that you're concerned with our past and he's interested in our present and future." He paused. "Trust me, David—this man can do important things for us."

"All right," I said. "I have no reason to doubt you. What's the problem?"

"What did you think it is?" he said irritably. "Those hidebound fools on the Council of Elders don't want him to come here."

"I thought they weren't invoking the fifty percent rule until we were fully populated," I said. "We can still handle another seven or eight thousand immigrants, possibly even a few more."

"They're opposed to him because he has no Maasai blood at all."

"This doesn't make sense," I said, shaking my head. "I know for a fact that they accepted a family of Zulus last month, and they certainly had no Maasai blood. And two Mtabele immigrated here the month before that, and—"

"Damn it, David!" snapped Joshua. "Open your eyes! It isn't his blood. It's his *color*!"

"There is nothing in our charter that says whites can't immigrate to Kilimanjaro," I said.

"There is nothing in our charter that says the Council of Elders has to behave like reasonable human beings and accept him either," said Joshua. "But if they don't, it won't take long before there's a backlash. Not only will no whites want to *live* here, but those who service our master computers, who help us clone our animals, who export the materials we need to expand our cities, will refuse to come here to a world of bigots. This could drive all white investment away."

"It's possible," I agreed.

"I'll be representing him before the Council," said Joshua. "I'd like your help."

"Freely given," I told him. "I don't give a damn about white backlashes or future economic investment. I'm only concerned with the morality of the situation, and if we are to be a Utopia, then it's clearly immoral to refuse this man the right to come here solely because of his color."

"Good. I knew I could count on you."

"Just be glad that I'm the only historian on Kilimanjaro," I said. "Because any historian could make the argument that this is merely a case of payback. The whites discriminated against the blacks for centuries, even buying and selling us as slaves at one point."

"That was all hundreds of years ago," he said impatiently.

"My job is to study what happened hundreds of years ago," I replied.

"I'm more concerned with what will happen next week," said Joshua. "This is a brilliant man, a decent man, who wants only to live out his remaining years here studying us and codifying what he learns for future generations—including future generations of Maasai. Consider that, David: most of your knowledge of our people, until the last two centuries, comes from European and Arab accounts. We had no written language, no interest in preserving our history. Now we not only have an official historian"—he nodded toward me—"but we have a chance to play permanent host to one of the leading sociologists on Earth. It would be folly to refuse to let him live here."

"You don't have to convince me," I said. "I have no problem with anyone living here, always excepting felons. It's Robert ole Meeli and the Council that you've got to convince."

"I know, I know," he said wearily. "My problem is that there's no higher court I can appeal to, and I know that the Council is already set against allowing Blumlein to come here."

"Could he come as a visitor?" I asked.

"A visitor?" he repeated, frowning.

"A tourist."

"We don't have a tourist industry," said Joshua. "Where would he stay?"

"There must be empty houses and apartments in any of the five cities," I said, "or we'd already be closed to immigration. Or perhaps he'd like to live with the pastoralists in the *manyattas*. Surely it would take almost no effort to build a *boma* for him."

"We don't have any rules for visitors," said Joshua. "I'm sure that if a Maasai wished to visit members of his family here, the Council would have no problem allowing it, and that would be a precedent. But they're hearing my argument for allowing William Blumlein to immigrate in just a few days, and I can't arrange for such a ruling before he arrives."

"I'll do what I can," I said. "But you're the lawyer. I don't know what arguments I can bring to your case, because as I say almost all of history suggests that we've been badly used by the white race and owe it nothing."

"And yet you're an historian and don't believe that," he said.

"I believe we've been badly used," I responded. "I don't believe William Blumlein, or any person now alive on Earth or in the Eutopian colonies, is responsible for it."

"I hope you can make that case to the Council."

"I don't argue before the Council," I said. "*You* are the lawyer. I'm the historian. You will do the speaking."

"Thanks," he said sarcastically.

"I'll do my best to help you prepare your case," I told him. "That's what you really want, and what I'll provide."

"Fair enough," he said. "Blumlein is due to arrive on Kilimanjaro tomorrow. Perhaps you'd like to come to my house for dinner?"

"I'll have to think about it," I said.

"What's to think about?" asked Joshua.

"What if I don't like him?" I responded.

"You'll do your best to help me anyway, not because you like or dislike him, but because we both know it's the right thing to do," he said with certainty. "I'll expect you at nightfall."

"All right," I said. "I'll be there."

I spent the rest of the day and the next morning studying the history, not of Kilimanjaro, which is not yet four years old, but of Kirinyaga and the other Eutopian worlds. I paid special attention to their immigration policies, looking for historical if not legal precedents.

William Blumlein had already arrived when I showed up at Joshua's house, which seemed divided equally between ancient law books that he never read since they were all more easily accessed on his computer, and an endless series of scientific gadgets that he would buy on impulse and never touch again once he'd brought them home. Blumlein was a pudgy white-haired man in his fifties, with a thick mustache and a ready smile. His manner immediately put me at my ease, and I remained that way through the dinner, though it was apparent that his intellect was truly prodigious. Everything interested him, and he seemed to have acquired at least some minimal knowledge on almost every conceivable subject.

I liked him, and I hated the thought of Kilimanjaro losing such a potentially worthwhile addition to our society. The problem was that I had no idea how to convince the Council to change their minds. They already knew his credentials and his reputation, and they still didn't want to allow him to live on our world.

I spent the next two days putting together a list of the most liberal immigration policies of the past five hundred years, then eliminated those where good intentions had not worked out. I had my computer transmit the information to Joshua, then I spent my free time showing Blumlein around the city and taking him out to the nearer *manyattas* while Joshua worked on his arguments.

"Fascinating!" exclaimed Blumlein as we drove back to the city from the last of the *manyattas*. "They're living the life they lived centuries ago, and feel no need to accommodate to the advances that are so apparent in the cities."

"We fought against the Westernization of our culture for centuries," I pointed out. "Kilimanjaro is three and a half years old."

"Ah, but these are not Europeans and Arabs and Indians living in your cities, enemy races or races to be shunned. These are Maasai enjoying those advantages. I think it's interesting that *any* Maasai choose to remain on the *manyattas*, without electricity or running water or modern medicine, especially when they can see their kinsman living comfortably in the cities."

"I'm sure you'll find an explanation for it," I said, "and then some future member of my profession will tell others of your conclusions."

"In other words, you have no opinion," he said with a twinkle in his eye.

"Everyone has opinions," I replied. "I have no facts."

"Well said!"

And somehow, despite my degrees and my accumulated honors, that seemed like the highest compliment I had ever received, if only because of who offered it.

I would have thanked him, but by then he was discussing the ersatz termite mounds and rocky outcrops, and trying to determine exactly how Maintenance had constructed them.

We reached the city at dusk, and the next morning I accompanied Joshua and Blumlein to the hearing. There was only one observer—Ledama, who sat like a statue, staring straight ahead with the hint of a frown on her face.

"Is she involved in this?" I whispered to Joshua just before he arose to address the Council.

"No," he said. "She sits here every day and raises bloody hell whenever the Council makes a decision that she thinks is wrong, which is most of the time. I doubt that she even knows what appeals they're listening to today."

Then he began stating his case and making his arguments, but to absolutely no avail. It was a travesty that made me ashamed of my own people. Here was a man who was willing to do and pay whatever was required to become a citizen, who was certain to create a classic study of Kilimanjaro and the Maasai, who asked for no special treatment—and Robert ole Meeli and the others were unmoved by his sincerity or Joshua ole Saibull's arguments.

I could see the decision slipping away, and so could Joshua, but there was nothing he could do about it. The Council was armored in its ignorance and its biases, and William Blumlein was going to spend the rest of his life bringing fame to some other culture.

A lunch break was called, and Joshua, Blumlein and I ate outside on a patio.

"They're not going to budge," complained Joshua. "They paid no attention to any of my arguments."

"Then there's no hope?" asked Blumlein.

"I'm afraid not," replied Joshua. "Oh, we'll go through the motions. I'll speak for most of the afternoon and probably tomorrow morning. I'll have David explain the historic reasons for allowing open immigration, and I've got holographic testimony from your peers explaining why your presence will be a boon to any society, but it's not going to work."

"Damn!" muttered Blumlein. "Is there nothing else we can try?"

"Yes," said Joshua disgustedly. "Go out in traffic and get hit by a car. If we use enough Maasai blood in the transfusion, they can't say you don't belong. Otherwise..."

"Just a minute," I said. "Say that again."

"Say *what* again?" demanded Joshua.

"If he had a large enough transfusion…"

"He'd be a Maasai by their own ruling," said Joshua. "But surely you aren't suggesting that William walk out in traffic in order to…"

"No," I said. "But you've given me an idea. First I need to ask a question." I turned to Blumlein. "Are you married?"

"Widowed," he replied.

"How badly do you want to be a citizen?"

"*Very* badly," said Blumlein.

Joshua spent most of the afternoon finding new ways of presenting the same arguments, while I sat in the back of the chamber, toying with the notion that had occurred to me. Then we were through for the day, the Council chambers were cleared, and Joshua walked Blumlein to his car. I lagged behind, and when I saw Ledama come out of the building I walked over to her.

"Good afternoon," I said pleasantly.

"Do you think so?" she snapped. "These fools are about to deny citizenship to a man any world would be proud to claim as its own!"

"Well, we have our traditions, and they have to maintain them. After all, he has no Maasai blood."

"We have others here who have no Maasai blood," she said angrily.

"But Zulus and Mtebele and other Africans have undergone the circumcision ritual."

"Are you trying to tell me that a white man with a name like Blumlein has not been circumcised?" she demanded.

"No," I said. "I just wish there was some way he could become a Maasai."

"No one *becomes* a Maasai," she said harshly. "You are born one or you are not. It's as simple as that."

"Yes, I suppose so," I said. "After all, it's not as if he'd been carried off in a raid and forced to wed a Maasai."

She stopped and stared at me, and I could see that the notion had registered.

"It was a silly suggestion," I said. "Such raids ended centuries ago, and besides, he's not a woman to be made one of a warrior's wives."

She seemed lost in thought and again made no reply, and I walked over to where Joshua and Blumlein were waiting in the car.

"What was *that* all about?" asked Joshua.

"I momentarily became a farmer," I responded.

"What are you talking about?"

"I planted a seed in the most fertile ground on Kilimanjaro," I said. "Tomorrow morning we will see if it has sprouted roots and grown."

"I understand *laibonis*, who deal only with the supernatural," complained Joshua. "Why is it that historians and sociologists speak in riddles?"

Blumlein laughed heartily at that, offered a funny rejoinder, and the subject was forgotten.

The next morning, as the Council seated themselves, Joshua was about to rise and speak to them, but he felt a heavy hand on his shoulder, holding him down. It belonged to Ledama, who approached Robert ole Meeli.

"What is it this time?" he said wearily, as if this was a common occurrence, and for all I knew it may have been.

"We have business to discuss," she announced.

"It can wait," replied Robert. "We are hearing the case of William Blumlein now."

"This has bearing on it," said Ledama firmly. "The Council will hear me first."

"But—" began Robert.

"Or do you want it known that you will no longer allow a woman to address the Council?" she continued.

He sighed deeply. "Speak, Ledama, daughter of Ntaiya."

"I thought that Kilimanjaro was supposed to be a Utopia," she began.

"We are doing our best to make it so," replied Robert.

"You have made it so for half the population," she responded. "The male half."

"What now?" he asked in goaded tones.

"How many wives do you have, Robert ole Meeli?" asked Ledama.

"Three," he said.

"Why?" she asked.

He seemed genuinely puzzled. "Why?" he repeated. "Because I wanted them, and could afford the bride price."

"Because you wanted them," she repeated.

"Yes."

"How many husbands may a Maasai woman have?"

"One."

"You see?" she said triumphantly. "Kilimanjaro cannot be a Utopia for women if you can have something we cannot have."

"We can shave our faces, and you cannot. You can have babies, and we cannot. There are many things only one sex can do. Perhaps you should take your petition to En-kai, who created us with all these differences."

"You are talking about differences we are born with, and cannot be changed. I am talking about *rights* that you have granted yourself, as a man, and refuse to grant me, as a woman."

And suddenly Joshua was at her side.

"Her petition has merit," he said, "and I wish to speak on her behalf."

He leaned over and whispered something to her—I found out later that he was assuring her that there would be no charge—and she quickly nodded her assent.

It took two full days, but when it was over the Council had agreed that to truly be a Utopia, Kilimanjaro must either practice monogamy for everyone, and since that clearly was not acceptable to the polygamous Council members, then polyandry must exist side-by-side with polygamy.

The next morning Ledama, who was already married, took William Blumlein as her second husband. They agreed that she would remain a city-dweller while he would spend his time living with and studying the pastoralists, but the mere act of marriage made him as much a Maasai as those kidnapped Kikuyu and Nandi women of centuries past.

The next morning Robert ole Meeli retired as the chief of the Council of Elders and within a week had returned to his ancestral home on Kenya's Loita Plains.

5 Afternoon on Kilimanjaro (2238 A.D.)

We should have seen it coming.

When Robert ole Meeli departed for Kenya, that left the Council of Elders divided with six men and six women. It was only a matter of a few days before the Council met to name a successor—and only a matter of a few minutes thereafter that Ledama, daughter of Ntaiya, and Ashina, daughter of Kibibi, led a march of literally hundreds of women demanding that the new Council member be a woman.

Ordinarily this would have been dealt with by a seven-to-six vote—but with Robert gone, there were six men and six women on the Council, and of course they were deadlocked.

Every day for a week the women (and after the first day, the men as well) presented their arguments, and every day the vote remained tied, six-to-six.

I knew it was only a matter of time until I was called before the Council of Elders, and in fact it took exactly six days.

"David ole Saitoti," said Martin ole Sironka, who was presiding over the meeting, "are you aware of why you have been summoned?"

"Since I have nothing else to offer," I replied, "I assume you seek my expertise as an historian."

"That is correct," said Martin. "And surely you are aware of the problem that confronts us."

"I am aware of it."

"How was this problem resolved in times past?" he continued.

"This particular problem was never resolved," I answered.

"What?" he demanded. "Surely in the long history of the Maasai…"

"It was never resolved, because it has never before occurred," I explained. "No woman ever sat on the Council of Elders before we came to Kilimanjaro."

"So there is nothing in our history to guide us?"

"There is nothing in *Maasai* history," I answered. "But it is possible that we can be guided by the histories of other races."

"How?" asked Martin.

"The Council of Elders rules Kilimanjaro, does it not?" I said.

"Of course it does," he said impatiently.

"What you must remember is that not all tribes and not all races have always had a Council of Elders or its equivalent," I continued. "In the earliest recorded history, most people were ruled by a king or chief, who achieved primacy either by inheriting it from his parents or through feats of physical strength, which frequently involved killing the previous ruler."

"Surely you're not suggesting that applicants to the Council of Elders must fight to prove their worthiness!" he snapped.

I shook my head. "No, Martin ole Sironka, I am not suggesting that. I'm merely telling you how leaders were chosen in ancient times."

"I don't see what that has to do with us," he grumbled.

"I'll try to show you," I said. He glared at me with a look that said: *Then get on with it or stop wasting my time.* "One of the problems with a single ruler, be he a king or chief or warlord, is that

·he frequently cannot make an informed decision. After all, one man can't know everything that is happening in his domain at any given moment."

"And this is how the Council of Elders came about?" asked another member.

"This is how *governments* came about," I said. "Kingdoms and countries became too complex for one man to rule, and so they were ruled by many men, though there was usually one man whose word was final. Sometimes these groups of men were called Councils of Elders, sometimes parliaments, sometimes congresses, sometimes other things."

"Then you haven't solved our problem at all," snapped Martin. "You have merely shown that every society has the same problem."

"I haven't finished," I said.

"You are very long-winded," he complained.

"That's because I have a lot of history to cover," I replied. "Now, as I was saying, there comes a time in the life of every society where one man can no longer rule it, and at that point there is created a ruling body of men, whether a Council of Elders or something else. But," I continued, "not every ruling body is responsible to the people it was created to rule. For example, let us assume that the next member of the Council is a city-dweller, as Robert ole Meeli was. Let us then assume that the pastoralists feel they are not being paid enough for their cattle, and petition the Council for a higher rate. And let us finally assume that, being human, the members of the Council vote for what is in their self-interest. There will be at least ten votes against the pastoralists, won't there?"

"Of course," said Martin. "What is your point, David ole Saitoti?"

"Simply this: that over the centuries the definition of the Councils and the parliaments and other bodies changed."

"In what way?"

"It was finally understood that their true purpose was not to rule, but to *serve*."

"Semantics!" he snorted contemptuously. "We *do* serve."

"But if you'll consider the example I offered, you are not serving the interests of the pastoralists who come to you for help. You are serving only your own interests—so why should they come to you at all?"

"Because we are the Council of Elders," he replied. "They have no other recourse."

"They have one," I said calmly. "And throughout history, whenever they feel they have been abused or ignored by the people that rule them, they have used it."

"And what is that?"

"Revolution," I said.

"We will hear no more of this!" yelled Martin, getting to his feet and leaving the chamber. Two men and a woman left with him— but eight members of the Council did *not* leave.

"Have there been many revolutions?" asked Isaac ole Olkejuado.

"There used to be."

"But no longer?"

I shook my head. "They've become increasingly rare."

"How were they prevented?" he asked.

"By making governments responsible for their actions," I said.

He seemed puzzled. "How?"

"Primarily by holding elections and letting the people decide who rules them," I answered. "And by doing it on a regular basis, so if one of the leaders—most people do not like the word *rulers*—isn't responsive to the needs of the people he's been elected to serve, he can be removed from office without violence and without revolution.

If a leader constantly votes in his own self-interest, he'll be voted out of office by the people he's supposed to serve, and that is definitely *not* in his self-interest. He will always keep that in mind."

"There were elections in Kenya," said Isaac. "This never concerned us, because the Kikuyu and Luo always won. They ignored us and we ignored them."

"The Kikuyu and Luo will not win an election on Kilimanjaro," I pointed out.

"We'll assemble the full Council here tomorrow morning, and you will make your case to us," said Isaac. "But don't be too hopeful, for what you are doing is asking us to put our futures in someone else's hands."

"As supplicants do every time they appear before the Council of Elders," I said.

"Save your arguments for tomorrow," he said. "We'll listen to them then."

And, surprisingly, they *did* listen. They asked a lot of questions and voiced a lot of objections, but they listened. I think it was the thought of revolution that finally encouraged them to agree to elections.

"That is the easy part," I announced when they were through congratulating each other. "Now you must write a constitution."

"Why?" asked Martin ole Sironka, who had been the one Council member to vote against allowing anyone else to vote.

"You must have a document that will define the duties—and especially the limitations—of those who are elected. It must state how much time will elapse between elections, and it must describe how the business of the Council is to be carried out. Do you remember the arguments you had about immigration a year ago? You've got to try to foresee every future problem, and if you can't solve them in the constitution, you must at least give the elected officials some guidelines for solving them."

"Is that all?" said Isaac sardonically.

"More will occur to you," I replied.

And more did.

Finally, after a month, the Council announced that they had completed work on their constitution, and would soon put it before the people for their approval.

"Don't you want to examine it and explain what they might have done wrong?" I asked that evening, as Joshua ole Saibull and I had dinner at a small restaurant.

"Why bother?" he said. "It's legal."

"What if it borrows from the old tradition that one mother cannot produce two souls? That if she produces twins one of them must be a demon—and not knowing which, the family is justified in killing them both."

"Let's hope they know better," said Joshua.

"What if there's something equally foolish in there, and they *don't* know better?" I persisted.

"You don't seem to understand, David," he said, pouring himself a beer. "This isn't a law or a tradition we're talking about. It's a constitution, the highest legal document on Kilimanjaro. If it says the buffalo in the game parks can vote and grown men can't, then that's the law."

"But—" I began.

"You're the historian, David," he interrupted. "Give me an honest answer. Did Adolph Hitler or any member of the Third Reich ever break German law?"

"They were illegal laws," I protested.

"You didn't answer my question," said Joshua.

I was silent for a long moment. "This could be a disaster," I said at last.

He shrugged. "People get the governments they deserve."

"To use your own example, did German Jews get the government or the laws *they* deserved?" I shot back.

"All right, David," he replied. "Tomorrow I'll look at the constitution."

He wasn't the only one to look at it. Ledama harangued the Council until they explicitly stated that women could run for any office. This so impressed young Mawenzi ole Porola that he led a children's march on the Council chambers protesting their making the minimum voting age 16 years, and got them to amend it so that anyone who had reach adulthood—which would be interpreted as having been circumcised—would be entitled to vote, and only those (more and more each year) who elected not to undergo the ritual would have to wait until they were 16 to vote. William Blumlein had been such a model citizen, friendly to all, and a major cash contributor to all five hospitals, that the immigration guidelines were relaxed still further. And of course polygamy and polyandry were written into the document.

Soon people were marching in front of the Council chamber every day, protesting some item in the proposed constitution or demanding that something else be inserted into it. This group wanted Maa to be the official language of Kilimanjaro; that group wanted to expand the cities and felt they could never attract off-world investment unless the official language was English. One group wanted to bring back mandatory circumcision; another group wanted it totally outlawed. Still another group wanted to get rid of the two game parks and provide more pastureland for the cattle; a rival group wanted not only to keep the parks, but to expand them so that we could clone elephants, which the current parks could not sustain.

It was when they began posting signs in the ground that Isaac ole Olkejuado sought me out.

"This has gotten out of hand, David," he complained.

"What do you mean?" I asked.

"Look around you!" he said. "Vote Yes! Vote No! Demand this! Protest that! Signs everywhere. Marchers picketing the Council. This isn't Kilimanjaro—it's Europe!"

"It's people expressing their views," I replied.

"It's more than that," he argued. "This is supposed to be a Maasai Utopia, not a British or French or American one!"

"I have learned two things from my study of Kirinyaga," I answered. "The first is that you can't stop a society from evolving."

"And the other?"

"That you can't always predict or control the direction in which it evolves."

"Is *this* what you want?" he insisted. "Men and women wearing Western clothes, walking up and down paved streets, politicking like Europeans, then going home to air-conditioned houses and apartments. Is this the Maasai Utopia?"

"Would you rather have them penniless, living in huts made of dung, covered by flies, totally ignorant of science and medicine?" I shot back.

"Of course not!" he snapped. "But there must be a middle ground!"

"Who chooses it?" I asked. "You?"

"Why not?" he said uneasily. "I am a member of the Council of Elders."

"And if the Council of Elders had been responsive to the needs of all the people that it's supposed to serve, do you think they'd be marching in front of your chambers day and night?" I asked.

"Well, damn it!" he said. "*You're* the one who convinced us to write a constitution and change the way Kilimanjaro works. What is *your* vision of a Maasai Utopia?"

"A world on which the Maasai have agreed upon the way they will live."

"But we *had* it!"

"Things change," I said. "Worlds change. Societies change."

"But this was the society we agreed to when we came here!" he complained.

"Did Ashina agree to being refused a place on the Council of Elders?" I replied. "Did Samuel, Mawenzi's father, agree to repeat a ritual that killed his first son? Did Ledama agree that she could identify herself only by a single name? Look around you, Isaac— Kilimanjaro is *already* evolving. I have not seen William Blumlein in three or four months, since before this situation occurred, but I'll wager he tells you that it is absolutely natural."

"What does he know?" Isaac shot back. "He is no Maasai."

"He is married to a Maasai," I said. "What would *you* call him?"

"A white intruder."

I shook my head. "He is a Maasai. Your own Council has said so."

He seemed about to argue, then turned on his heel and walked away.

Word had gotten to Blumlein, and he had left his *manyatta* and come to the city, where he seemed omnipresent, observing, questioning, making endless notes on his pocket computer. I even saw him having lunch one day with Ledama, probably the first time they'd met since their marriage.

One day I happened to be passing a small public park, not a game park, just an acre of green breaking up the cement of the city, and I saw him sitting on a bench. He was alone, and not dictating into his machine, so I walked over and greeted him.

"Hello, David," he said. "Have a seat. Isn't it fascinating?"

"I'd have thought it was entirely predictable," I said, sitting down next to him.

"Oh, eventually it had to happen—but so *soon*! It's really quite remarkable." He glanced at me out of the corner of his eye. "I suspect you are to thank for it."

"You heard?"

He shook his head. "No. But who else would speak to the Council of elections and constitutions?"

"Why not Joshua?" I suggested.

"Joshua and the other lawyers know the law as it is being practiced. Why suggest something that would require them to re-learn their profession? No, my friend, it had to be you."

"It was me," I admitted. "But only after I was asked."

"There's no blame involved, David," he said. "This is the direction all societies take, some faster, some slower, some with more complexity, some with less." He smiled. "Some with unbelievable violence, some with none at all."

"*All* societies?" I asked dubiously.

He nodded his head. "Most hit enough bumps in the road that you can't recognize it at first, but universal suffrage and universal equality, of opportunity if not position, is the eventual goal of every society."

"Based on your observations, how is this one doing?" I asked.

He shrugged. "It's too soon to tell. There are half a hundred ways to temporarily derail it, but the operative word is *temporary*. Usually when they evolve this quickly, the change is accompanied by violence, because usually the entrenched powers are not prepared to bow to the inevitable. But Kilimanjaro was based on the Maasai society of Earth, where most of these problems had already been worked out, so I have hope."

"That gives *me* hope," I said.

"You? You're the historian," he said with a laugh. "None of this should surprise you."

"I deal with results, not with the processes that lead to the results," I explained.

"Good old David," he said. "You always have a rational answer to things."

"Thank you. I think."

"Yes, it's a compliment," he said. "Sort of. Tell me, have they settled on a title for whoever's going to run the whole place?"

"Just Leader, as far as I know," I said.

"Not *laibon*?" he asked. "Maasai chiefs were always *laibons*."

I shook my head. "It is too close to *laiboni*. We wouldn't want outsiders to think we were voting to be ruled by a witch doctor."

"Actually, Leader is a pretty good name for it," he replied. "You have to watch out for the ones who give the job grandiose titles." He paused, staring at a mob of pastoralists who marched by, carrying signs demanding the elimination of the game parks. "Has anyone announced for the office yet?"

"Not to my knowledge," I said. "Though I've heard that Ashina is considering running for it."

"I'd ask if she has any experience," said Blumlein, "but it's a stupid question. No one has any experience. I've suggested to Joshua that he toss his hat into the ring."

"What did he say?" I asked.

Blumlein grinned. "That if I ever mentioned it again, he'd throw me all the way back to Earth."

I chuckled at that. "Obviously being a lawyer pays better than being a ruler."

"As long as there are at least two lawyers in town," agreed Blumlein.

We chatted for a few more minutes, and then I got up and returned to my office.

The picketing and politicking went on for another two weeks, and some minimal changes were made in the constitution, but finally the Council decided it was time for an up-or-down vote, and it won by a large majority.

Then it was time to elect the Council members. Most of them won quite handily, since they were running on the basis of experience. Still, it was apparent that they were expected to be more responsive to their constituents this time, or they would be looking for work after the next election.

That left only the position of Leader. As I had predicted, Ashina announced her candidacy. When word of what had transpired reached Kenya, Robert ole Meeli actually returned to Kilimanjaro to run for Leader. Isaac ole Olkejuado decided to run as well, and soon there were no less than fourteen announced candidates.

If Isaac had thought the streets were noisy and crowded before, when people were campaigning for the constitution, he must had been driven practically berserk by the new level of noise and activity. Every candidate had his or her supporters, and not only were the streets filled with marchers, but with cattle, as the pastoralists, unwilling to leave their herds unattended, drove them through the towns to voice their support of one candidate or another.

Blumlein was there every day, looking positively delighted with the developments. People who had stared at his unusual white face months earlier now took him for granted, as if he were part of the urban landscape, as indeed he had become.

"Tell me the truth, William," I said one afternoon, as we were watching yet another herd of cattle walking down the middle of our main thoroughfare, with a candidate's name written on their sides in white paint. "You couldn't have foreseen this when you arrived."

"No," he admitted. "But isn't it wonderful? For more than a century the Maasai didn't give a damn who ruled Kenya, as long as they got to graze their cattle and live in their *manyattas*. They had no more interest in voting than in cross country skiing. But now look at these herders!"

"Do they even know the issues, I wonder?" I mused aloud.

"They know who's promised to raise the price on cattle," he answered. "They know who's promised to get rid of the game parks. They know who's promised free health care for their children. They don't know the other 57 issues, but why should they? They know the ones they care about."

He had a point. Everyone knew the issues they cared about. The city dwellers and the pastoralists, the merchants and the students, the wealthy and the poor, the members of each of the five clans. And they knew which candidates addressed those issues that most concerned them.

And that was getting us nowhere. We had no pollsters, of course, but I was convinced that none of the fourteen candidates could capture as much as fifteen percent of the vote. This had not been anticipated by the constitution: it simply claimed that the winner would be the candidate with the most votes, rather than the one with a majority of the votes, so it was possible that our first Leader could actually lose 85% of the vote.

Two days before the election it was arranged for each of the candidates to address the same audience on the outskirts of the largest of our cities. Each got up and made his or her promises, and each received raucous applause from a tiny section of the audience and polite applause from the rest.

I looked at the assembled candidates. Each was well-meaning, none had had an opportunity to become corrupt yet, all believed in Kilimanjaro or they wouldn't be here…and yet they seemed to fade together, all pastels, no primaries. What we needed was a Batian or a Nelion, two great Maasai of the past for whom the peaks of

Kirinyaga—Mount Kenya—had been named. What we had were fourteen well-meaning people who were not prepared to lead this world, small as it was.

Finally I could stand it no longer, so I stepped up on the platform from which each candidate had addressed the audience.

"Are you announcing your candidacy, David ole Saitoti?" asked Martin ole Sironka.

"No," I said. "I am not qualified to be the Leader of Kilimanjaro."

"Then why are you standing there?"

"Because there is a man who is uniquely suited to be our Leader," I said. "He is the most educated man on Kilimanjaro. He doesn't belong to any of the five clans, so he won't favor one over the other. He isn't a city dweller, so he won't favor the cities over the herders. He isn't a herder, so he won't favor them over the city-dwellers. He has seen how societies evolve, and he can guide us along the proper path. Finally, the Council of Elders has ruled that he is a Maasai." I stared at the audience, hoping my candidate was not there so that he couldn't instantly withdraw. "He is William Blumlein."

There was no applause. There were no cheers. But I noticed that there were a lot of whispered discussions going on as I stepped down from the platform.

Each of the fourteen candidates in turn ascended the platform to denounce my choice, explaining that he would not do for their constituency what they could do. But each time one of them spoke, he or she alienated the nine out of ten Maasai who were *not* their constituents.

The election was held two days later, and Blumlein, the white Maasai, won more than seventy percent of the vote. A steer was slaughtered in his honor, and we held a victory feast that lasted well into the night. Finally, when he was sure no one could overhear him, he leaned over to me and whispered: "You son of a bitch! I spent all day yesterday arguing with the Council. The constitution doesn't provide a way for a candidate to withdraw! You knew that!"

"Can you think of a better candidate?" I asked him.

"That's beside the point."

"Not any longer," I replied. "You're a Maasai, and a citizen of Kilimanjaro. That *is* the point."

"I'll have to find a role for you in my government," he said with an evil smile.

"Every position is already filled," I answered. "But I'll be happy to write the history of your reign."

"You're screwing up this society's evolution," he said seriously. "Don't you realize that?"

"You're *part* of this society," I said. "Don't *you* realize that?"

"Good old David," he said in resignation. "Always a rational answer."

The next morning Blumlein took office. He made a hell of a speech, too. And I found myself thinking: *Poor Darwin. He only got to see the aftermath of evolution. I'm going to get to watch it in action.*

6 TWILIGHT ON KILIMANJARO (2239 A.D.)

I was sitting at my computer, proofreading a paper I had prepared on the earliest days of Kilimanjaro, when the machine spoke up.

"David ole Saitoti, your presence is required at the local hospital."

"Can you give me any details?" I asked it.

"You are expected," said the computer. "Someone will greet you."

I didn't know if it was an emergency or not, so I decided it would be better to drive there in my own car than to take public transportation. I went down to the garage, got into my vehicle, and sped to the hospital, which was about two miles away. I left the car with an attendant, then rushed into the lobby. No one was waiting for me, so I went up to the registration desk.

"I am David ole Saitoti," I said. "I received a message that—"

"Ah, yes," said the receptionist. "Your presence is requested in room 208."

"Is it Joshua ole Saibull?" I asked. "Or perhaps Leader Blumlein?"

"I don't know," she replied. "I only know that you are to report to room 208."

I took an airlift to the second level, then walked down the corridor until I came to the room in question. I opened the door and entered it. An emaciated old man lay on the bed, bandages and dressings on his right arm, tubes running into and out of his body. A doctor walked over to greet me.

"You're David ole Saitoti?" he asked.

"Yes."

"I'm glad you could come so quickly."

"Why am I here?" I asked. "I don't know this patient."

"He requested your presence."

"He did?" I said, surprised. I stared intently at the old man. "I've never seen him before. Perhaps you misunderstood him."

"I doubt it," replied the doctor. "You're the historian, aren't you?"

"Yes."

"He insisted that we summon an historian." He smiled. "It was an easy choice. You seem to be the only one we have."

I looked down at the patient. "What's the matter with him?"

"He tried to kill himself" was the answer. "He botched the job. I think we'll probably release him tomorrow."

"But all these tubes..." I said.

"Just precautions. He was dehydrated, and his electrolyte balance was poor."

"Why did he try to take his own life?" I asked.

"I have no idea," said the doctor. "I think that's what he wants to talk to you about."

"What's his name?"

The doctor looked at a hand computer. "Sokoine ole Parasayip."

"Never heard of him."

"Well, you have now." Something beeped in one of his pockets. "I've got to go down the hall," he said. "I'll be back in a few minutes."

He left the room, and I turned back to the patient, who was now staring unblinking at me.

"I thought you were asleep," I said, startled.

"I was awake," he replied. "I simply had nothing to say to the city *laiboni*."

"He's not a witch doctor," I said.

"Of course he is. I practice the ancient ways, he practices the new ways. Otherwise we are the same."

"So you're a *laiboni*?"

"I am a *laiboni*," confirmed Sokoine ole Parasayip. He stared at me. "You look puzzled."

"I am," I told him.

"Why?"

"Two reasons," I said. "First, I don't know why a *laiboni* would want to kill himself. And second, why do you need an historian? I gather you asked for me by profession rather than by name."

"That is true," said Sokoine.

"Well?" I said.

"I find it very uncomfortable to speak with you while lying flat on this bed. Can you help me to my feet?"

"No," I said. "But I can raise the part beneath your pillow."

I reached over and adjusted the control, and the top quarter of his bed slowly rose until it was at a 45-degree angle with the rest of it.

"Better?" I asked.

"Much," said Sokoine.

I looked around, spotted a chair, summoned it to his bedside, and sat down on it. "Now perhaps you can tell me why a man I've never seen before, a man who just tried to kill himself, wants me to visit him."

"I must learn things that only an historian can tell me," he answered.

"What kind of things?"

"I am a *laiboni*," began Sokoine.

"So you said," I replied. "Where are you from?"

"The *manyattas* between the cities of *il-taarrosero* and *il-ikumai*."

"I know the area," I said.

"I am a good *laiboni*," he continued. "I have never done anything to bring disrespect or shame upon myself or my calling."

"Okay, you're a good *laiboni*," I replied. "What about it?"

"I have treated the sick, I have blessed the cattle, I have presided at the circumcision rituals and the Eunoto, the ceremony where the *elmoran* become junior elders. Whatever I have been requested to do I have done. If the family that made the request was poor, I have accepted only a single goat as my fee, not even an old steer. I am a good *laiboni*."

"Why does a good *laiboni* try to end his life?" I asked.

"What is a *laiboni* to do when he is no longer wanted or needed?" asked Sokoine miserably. "Not a single girl in my domain has been circumcised this year. Eleven boys have been circumcised, but here in the hospital, not in the traditional ceremony. I no longer am asked to bless the cattle, for the animal *laiboni*—the veterinarian—comes out from *il-ikumai* with his medicines. The children ignore me, the young men laugh at me, the elders look at me with the same sympathy as when they look at an old cow that will soon be slaughtered." He stared at me, his face a mask of puzzlement. "What is a *laiboni* to do when he is no longer needed?"

"What he shouldn't do is kill himself," I said.

"I have gone to other areas in the hope that *they* might need me. Those that already had *laibonis* told me to go away, and those that had none didn't want one. I spoke to some other *laibonis*, and they have the same problem. For untold generations the Maasai needed their *laibonis*. We were treated with dignity and respect, and our calling was honored above all others. And now, in the space of only a few years we have become useless old men, outcasts in our own land."

I didn't know what to say to him, so I simply reached out and held his hand.

"I am a coward," he continued after a brief pause. "The Maasai are supposed to fear nothing, yet I feared a meaningless life, so I tried to end it. I cut the veins in my arm *here*"—he indicated a place beneath the bandages on his forearm—"and was prepared to bleed to death, but two *elmoran* found me and carried me to this hospital. I suppose when I am released I will try again, but first I thought I would speak to an historian."

"I'm happy to speak to you," I said. "But what do you wish to discuss?"

"There is another Eutopian world that was colonized by a tribe from Kenya," he began.

"Yes, Kirinyaga," I said. "It was settled by the Kikuyu."

"And the Kikuyu have their *laibonis*, which they call *mundumugus*."

"That's right."

"Have you studied Kirinyaga, or merely the history of Earth?" he asked.

"I've studied Kirinyaga," I said unhappily, because I could tell what his next question was going to be.

"Tell me how the *mundumugus* fared on Kirinyaga, how they kept their people's respect, and perhaps I will be able to do the same here on Kilimanjaro."

"Kirinyaga is a different world," I said.

"They fared *that* badly?" he asked.

"There was only one *mundumugu*," I replied. "His name was Koriba. As far as I can tell, he was an honorable man, and he must have been an intelligent one, because he had advanced degrees from universities in England and America."

"But?" said Sokoine.

"But he was a fanatic," I said. "He was convinced that a Kikuyu Utopia could be achieved only by rejecting everything European, by living as the Kikuyu lived before any white men arrived in Kenya."

"He may have been right," said Sokoine.

"He was wrong," I said. "I've studied Kirinyaga's history. It is a series of well-meaning blunders, until even Koriba must have realized that he was harming his world, because eventually he returned to Kenya."

"And he was their only *mundumugu*?"

"Yes."

"Is it inevitable that every world will reject its spiritual leader, or is it only true of African worlds?" he asked curiously. "What of the Christian or Moslem Eutopias?"

"It's not so much that they rejected spiritual leadership, but rather that some of the people were more willing to accept new ideas than their spiritual leaders."

"What is new about medical doctors?" insisted Sokoine irritably. "They have been around for centuries."

"But the Maasai who lived on the savannah and tended their herds did not have access to them for centuries," I pointed out. "The Maasai who went to live in the cities have been using them for centuries."

Sokoine was quiet for a long time. I thought he'd fallen asleep again, but finally he spoke.

"I know why Koriba left Kirinyaga," he said.

"Why?"

"For the same reason I must leave Kilimanjaro," replied Sokoine. "He did not want to watch his god defeated by the god of the Westerners."

"It is the same god," I said. "We just give Him different names."

He shook his head. "En-kai has slowly been pushed out of Africa. I had hoped that this would be the world where He would finally triumph, but it is not to be. The God of the whites has won again." He sighed in resignation. "I must find the world that En-kai has retreated to."

"He's right where He has always been," I said. "Didn't He lead the two *elmoran* to you before you could bleed to death?"

"So that they could bring me to this...this *place*," he said contemptuously. "That is not the act of a compassionate god. No, historian, En-kai is no longer on Kilimanjaro."

I stared at the bitter old man. I'm an historian; it wasn't *my* job to convince him that life was worth living. But he had reached out to me, and I felt an obligation to try.

"Have you decided that it is your duty to find En-kai?" I asked, trying to order my thoughts.

"Yes," he answered. "All the Maasai are in Africa or on Kilimanjaro, so He must be very lonely on His new world, with no one to honor His wishes and worship Him."

"You're looking too far afield," I said.

"What do you mean?"

"En-kai wants you to find Him and worship Him, right?"

"Yes."

"You can't find him if you're dead," I said, and when I saw that he didn't follow my reasoning, I added: "If he wants you to worship Him, then he clearly wants you alive...so it was En-kai who directed the *elmoran* to find you and bring you here. And if He did that, then He is still on Kilimanjaro."

He stared long and hard at me, frowning. "There is a flaw in your argument, but I cannot see it."

"Perhaps you'd better remain on Kilimanjaro until you can," I suggested. "Until you know En-kai isn't here, there's no sense looking elsewhere for Him."

"I will consider it," he said.

"Good," I said. "I understand there's a chance the hospital will release you tomorrow. Have you got a place to stay?"

"I wander from *manyatta* to *manyatta*. No one refuses shelter to the *laiboni*. Although," he added, a trouble look on his wrinkled face, "that was before. Tomorrow they may decide they have no more use for a *laiboni*."

"You can stay at my place until you've recovered your strength," I said.

"Share a hut with a computer?" he said distastefully.

"It's not a hut," I replied. "And who knows? Maybe my computer can teach you a thing or two that will convince the Maasai that their *laiboni* is not an antique to be cast aside like an empty gourd."

He stared at me, unblinking. "Why are you doing this?" he asked at last. "You clearly have no use for a *laiboni*. You do not believe in my magic. You live in the city, you do not wear the red blanket, you carry no spear. Why would such a person help me?"

I had to think about my answer for a minute. Finally I spoke.

"Because I'm an historian, and men like you are part of our history."

"But not your future," he said bitterly.

"I don't know," I said. "Today won't be history until tomorrow. You'll have to ask me then."

"Now *that* is interesting," he said weakly. He seemed about to say something else, but suddenly his eyes closed and he lay still. For a moment I thought he had died, but all the machines that were monitoring him kept beeping quietly and I realized that he had simply fallen asleep.

They actually kept Sokoine for three days, until they were satisfied with his condition, and then they released him in my care. I drove him to my apartment, waited for the scanner to check my retina and bone structure, and then entered with him as the door slid into a wall, and then slid shut behind us.

"You're only my second house guest," I remarked as he looked around the place. "The first was also a visitor from the *manyattas*." I thought back on Mawenzi's one night there. "He thought the computer was magic."

"Alien to the Maasai, yes," said Sokoine. "Magic, no. Surely he saw computers in the ship that brought him here."

"He was just a young boy," I explained. "He probably didn't remember them, or pay them any attention. After all, he went right from a hut on the African savannah to a spaceship. It must have been an overwhelming experience."

"By now he probably wears a suit and tie, and looks upon the *manyattas* with contempt."

"He's still there with his cattle, and a new bride," I said. "I see him from time to time."

"He has seen the city, actually visited it, and he still prefers the life of a herder?" said Sokoine. "Perhaps there is some shred of hope yet."

I decided not to take him to the restaurant where I usually eat. An old man in his *laiboni* gear would attract too much attention, so I made dinner for us in my kitchen. He asked a lot of questions about the stove, the range, the freezer, and the other appliances. I could tell he wasn't thrilled with the meal, but he ate it without complaint. And without saying a word.

After dinner he sat in my living room, staring off into space, still silent. I read a bit, did a little work on the computer, and went to bed. When I awoke in the morning, he was still sitting there, motionless.

"Are you all right?" I asked as I approached him.

It took him a moment to realize I was there and to react to my presence. "Yes," he replied. "*Now* I am all right, thanks to what you said."

"What I said?" I repeated.

"That today would be history tomorrow. You were right, David ole Saitoti. Everything changes, and what seems new today is tomorrow's history. My job is to bring my people comfort, to scare away demons, to give them peace of mind." Suddenly he smiled. "It is history. Not the need to comfort my people, to heal their wounds and protect them from demons. That is eternal. But the *means* by which I performed my duties are clearly history. They have been replaced by new means—by medical doctors, by hospitals, by complex machines. And tomorrow *they* will be history, and the needs of my people will remain."

"You're right, of course," I said. "But I can't quite see what you're driving at."

"The means will always change," he said. "It is the *need* that is eternal. And since I am here today, I must use today's means to accomplish En-kai's purpose." He paused. "Today you will take me back to the hospital, not as a patient but as a student. *Laiboni* is just a word. It is what the *laiboni* does that matters."

"I know a couple of men who might be able to help," I said. I didn't mention that one of them was the Leader of the entire planetoid. "But I must warn you that if you are accepted, you will begin training as a practical nurse. You may find the work tedious and even demeaning after having been a *laiboni*."

He shrugged. "One must begin somewhere. It is not demeaning to help those in need. The only demeaning thing is not to try."

He was probably thirty years older than me, but I felt like a proud father as I drove him to the hospital.

It was enough to make me once again believe in En-kai.

Well, almost.

7 Night on Kilimanjaro (2240 A.D.)

I was awakened in the middle of the night. The vidphone kept calling my name, louder each time, until I finally swung my feet over the edge of the bed, sat up, reached over to the nightstand, and activated it.

"Yeah?" I mumbled. "What is it?"

"David, this is Joshua."

I peered at the holoscreen. "I can see that. What time is it?"

"Three-thirty in the morning."

"Whatever it is, it can wait," I said, about to break the connection and go back to sleep.

"Damn it, David!" he yelled, startling me. "Wake up!"

I rubbed my eyes with the backs of my hands. "All right, all right. I'm awake. Now why the hell are you calling me at three-thirty in the morning?"

"We need your expertise," said Joshua.

"I'm an historian, not a goddamned vampire hunter," I muttered. "Is this some kind of joke?"

"This is not a joke. This is a vitally important matter, and we need your expertise as an historian. Is that clear enough for you?"

"Who is *we?*" I asked, still trying to focus my eyes.

"The police and me."

"All right," I said again. "I'll get dressed and come…" I stopped, confused. "Where am I going—the police station or your office?"

"I want you to go to wherever you keep all your research," he said.

"It's in my office," I said. "That's three blocks away."

"Can you access it from your apartment?"

"I don't even know what I'm accessing," I complained.

"Take a minute, get your head on straight, grab a robe, and when I'm sure you're thinking clearly and not about to go back to sleep, I'll tell you about it."

I got up without saying another word and walked to the kitchen. Then I ordered a cup of coffee from the Galley Slave that I had installed a few months ago when I finally got sick of cooking. I listened as it hummed for a few seconds, and then took my cup of steaming hot coffee.

I wandered over to the kitchen table, sat down, ordered the vidphone extension to activate, and waited for Joshua's holograph to pop into existence.

"I'm up, I'm awake, and I'm caffeinated," I said. "Now what's so damned important that it couldn't wait until morning?"

"We've got a corpse here," said Joshua. "Well, not exactly *here*. I'm going to transmit holos of it to your home computer."

"I hope you don't expect me to look at holos of a dead body at four in the morning!" I said irritably.

"It's only three-thirty-five," he said. "And this isn't your typical dead body. It's been mutilated."

"Oh, that makes everything all right," I said. "This is some kind of practical joke, right?"

"No, David, it's not a joke. They have arrested my cousin, and I'm going to be defending him."

"Your cousin Moses, who's always getting drunk?"

"That's the one. Someone saw him wandering in the vicinity of the crime earlier in the evening, and when they picked him up and questioned him he couldn't remember a damned thing."

"I wish you luck," I said.

"I need more than luck," said Joshua. "I need your input."

"I'm an historian!" I snapped. "What the hell do I know about mutilated corpses?"

"I'm not sure," he said. "*Something*, I hope."

"All right," I said. "Man or woman?"

"Neither."

"I beg your pardon?"

"The proper question is: male or female? It's female."

"I don't understand."

"Someone sneaked into the game park about three hours ago—I haven't figured out how he breached the force field yet—but the end result is that he killed and mutilated a rhinoceros."

"A rhinoceros," I repeated stupidly.

He nodded affirmatively. "Killed her with a poisoned dart, and after she was dead the killer cut off her horns."

"You need a psychiatrist, Joshua, not an historian," I said.

"Perhaps," he acknowledged. "But I wanted to talk to you first. This wasn't a case of self-defense, David. It was premeditated."

"How do you know that?"

"Because you don't go walking around innocently at night, or any other time, with poisoned darts. Also, the killer stayed around long enough to cut off the horns—and very neatly, too. Clearly he didn't want to damage them. I can imagine someone being in a rage after barely escaping a rhino charge and somehow killing the animal...but then he wouldn't have been so meticulous cutting off the horns. So it's got to be premeditated."

"You make it sound like murder, with all this talk of killing and premeditation," I said. "All that happened is that someone destroyed public property."

"There has to be a reason, David. You don't risk your life against a rhino just for the hell of it." He paused. "I know that rhinos used to be abundant, and they were poached to near-extinction, primarily for their horns. But I need to know more. Does the horn represent some religious object? Is this some kind of ritual passage to adulthood, like when our *elmoran* were expected to kill a lion with a spear? Maybe the killer *is* just a nut case, but if there's any valid reason for his actions, it'll make it a lot easier to track him down if we understand it. Anyone can find out what we did to the rhinos; what I need to know is *why*. What was so special about a rhinoceros horn that people all but destroyed an entire species, and risked jail time to do it?"

"I'll see what I can find out," I said. "Are you *sure* your client is innocent?"

"Dead certain," he replied. "Hell, the police know he didn't do it. They just felt they had to arrest *someone*."

"I've got one last question."

"What is it?"

"Moses ole Kaelo hasn't had two shillings to rub together in years. How do you expect him to pay you?"

"You explain to me about rhinoceros killers and I'll explain to you about *pro bono* legal work," he said, signing off.

I toyed with going back to sleep, but I was too wide awake now, not from the coffee but from Joshua's notion that there might actually be a reason why someone would slaughter a rhinoceros and remove its horns.

I sat down at my computer and tried to order my thoughts. Since I wasn't as sharp as usual, I decided to use voice commands rather than the more exacting keystrokes.

"Computer, activate," I said.

Activated, it replied.

"Tie into all files in my office computer that are not sealed or protected by passwords."

Working...done.

"When did the last rhinoceros die?"

Working...The last African black rhinoceros died in 2067 A.D. The last African white rhinoceros died in 2061 A.D. The last Indian rhinoceros died in 2055 A.D. The last Sumatran rhinoceros—

"That's enough," I said. "Now I want you to check back through all African court records and see if anyone was ever arrested for killing a rhinoceros."

Working...13,671 people were arrested for poaching rhinoceri. The number of poached rhinoceri was between 861,000 and 864,000 during the 20th century, and 1,342 more since then.

"Why the discrepancy in 20th century numbers?" I asked.

It is due to the fact that up to 3,000 rhinoceri died from causes other than poaching and later had their horns removed by opportunistic men and women who chanced upon their corpses.

"Had any of those 13,671 people removed the rhinos' horns?"

13,494 of the people arrested for killing rhinoceri were charged with removing the horns.

"Computer, what was the reason for killing so many rhinos?"

To gain possession of the horns.

No surprise there. "And what was the reason for gaining possession of the horns?"

Profit.

"Who would pay for a rhino horn?"

In China, doctors prescribed powdered rhinoceros horn as a powerful aphrodisiac. In North African countries, the horn of the rhinoceros was used as the hilt of a dagger.

"What was a rhinoceros horn worth in Kenya shillings?"

Insufficient data. Since the value of both the horn and the shilling fluctuated, I must be given a time frame.

"All right. What was the value in 1980?"

From 22,000 to 30,000 Kenya shillings, depending upon the size and quality of the horn.

"And the shilling was worth how much?"

The rate of exchange in 1980 was 4.23 Kenya shillings to the British pound.

"What was the per capita income of the Kenyan citizen, regardless of tribe, in 1980?"

2,491.28 shillings per annum.

I was silent for a moment while I did the math in my head. No wonder they had killed almost a million rhinos! A dead rhino was worth an average of more than ten times what most Kenyans could earn in a year!

"Computer," I said at last, "is there a market for rhino horns today?"

The market is extremely limited because the horns are almost unattainable, but such rarities would clearly fetch prices well in excess of those that were obtained during the late 20th and early 21st centuries. Adjusting for inflation, a minimum price would be 625,000 shillings, probably far more if interested parties were allowed to bid against each other.

I contacted Joshua on the vidphone and told him what I had learned. He seemed unimpressed.

"I knew most of that, and surmised the rest," he said. "That's very disappointing news, David."

"I don't understand," I said.

"No one's making ceremonial knives any more," he said. "As for the horn being an aphrodisiac when it was ground up and sprinkled over your food or drink, I had my computer analyze it. You could get the same effect grinding up your fingernails and sprinkling *them* in your drink, which is to say: none at all." He grimaced. "That means it's strictly a collector's item from an extinct animal that's been cloned—and that means that every damned animal in the park is at risk. Hell, lions and leopards and impala have been extinct every bit as long as the rhino. A collector who wants a rhino horn simply because of its rarity may be just as interested in a hippo tooth, or a lion's mane, or a kudu horn—and there are probably a lot of collectors. If we don't put a stop to this right now, the poacher will strike again. After all, it's easy money, and it's *huge* money. And when word gets out, and it always does, we'll have more poachers."

"*Could* Moses have done it?"

"Not a chance," answered Joshua. "They found him on this side of the force field. Hell, Moses couldn't cross that field without killing himself on those rare occasions that he's sober. He certainly couldn't have done it tonight. As for shooting a dart accurately in the dark…"

"All right," I said. "Then it's an easy case and you'll get him off."

"I'm not concerned with case, damn it!" he half-yelled. "I'm concerned with catching the poacher and making sure it doesn't happen again so our game parks aren't overrun by them!"

He broke the transmission.

I thought of going back to bed, but now I was awake and alert, and it occurred to me that my job wasn't done yet. I knew how rhinos had been poached to the brink of extinction in the late 20th century—but the fact was that they had survived another fifty years. How?

"Computer?" I said.

Activated.

"What was the rhinoceros population of Kenya in 1950?"

103,625 black and 17 white.

"In 1970?"

72,133 black and 9 white.

"In 1990?"

428 black and no white.

Well, it was obvious when most of the poaching had been done.

"In 2010?"

1,238 black and 28 white.

So the black rhino, which seemed headed for immediate extinction in 1990, had tripled its number in the next twenty years. I asked the computer to explain this. It couldn't, so I got dressed and went to my office, activated my more powerful computer, and accessed files from Earth that were unavailable to my personal computer.

The answer was surprising yet, when I thought about it, inevitable. A few private sanctuaries and farms—Solio Ranch, Lewa Downs, a handful of others—had decided that the rhinos could not be saved in the national parks, so they began raising rhinos themselves.

And why didn't the same poachers kill them there?

That was the surprise.

The farms hired the very best protection money could buy—and that meant former poachers. They were given weapons, uniforms, salaries, living quarters, and respect, and it was this handful of reformed poachers who ensured the survival of the rhinoceros in Kenya for another half century, until the farms were finally sold to developers and the last bit of rhino habitat was lost.

Creating a solution to the embryonic problem on Kilimanjaro would take some innovation. As far as I knew we had only one poacher, and once we identified him we were certainly going to jail him, not hire him to stop other poachers from plying their trade.

But that didn't mean that we didn't have the makings of an anti-poaching squad. There were a lot of young men out on the pastoralists' land. Surely some of them must be bored with their lives.

Others must be having difficulty putting together the bride price for the woman they wanted to wed. Some might just be looking for, if not excitement, then at least a change in their lives, one that didn't involve moving to one of the cities.

I called for an appointment with William Blumlein the next day, and he made room in his schedule for me just before lunch.

"Good morning, William," I said as I was ushered into his office.

He sat behind his desk, looking very comfortable in a short-sleeved shirt and lightweight tan slacks.

"Hello, David," he said, rising and shaking my hand. "What can your government do for you today?"

"We have a problem," I said.

He arched an eyebrow sardonically. "In Utopia? Maybe I should have refused this job."

"I'm serious, William."

"Okay, tell me about it. I hope you don't mind if we capture it to holo. I do this with all my meetings. It saves my having to repeat everything to whatever department I turn it over to."

I filled him in on the situation. Before I could suggest my solution, he interrupted me.

"We're going to have to protect the parks," he said. "I know we've got force fields, but clearly someone has learned how to get past them, and if he isn't apprehended soon there's no reason to assume he won't pass the word to potential confederates. The way I see it, we're going to need park rangers, or game wardens, or whatever the hell we decide to call them.."

"I fully agree, sir," I said.

"Ideally, based on your research, we should go through our jail, approach each poacher, and offer to commute their sentences if they'll come to work for us. But we don't *have* any poachers in jail. So," he concluded, "what do you suggest?"

"We should hire the young men from the *manyattas*," I suggested. "I can't see hiring the city dwellers."

He shook his head. "It'll never work, David. They've never seen a wild animal in their lives. They would have no idea how to poach a rhino, so they will have no idea how to stop a poacher. Also, their currency is cattle, and I'm not equipped to pay them in cattle."

"Then are you just going to wait until he strikes again and hope you get lucky?" I asked rather angrily, annoyed that he had found so many holes in my solution so easily.

"You nominated me for this job, David. You should have a little more confidence in me."

"All right," I said. "What do you plan to do?"

"I can't hire poachers, because we only have one and we haven't caught him yet," answered Blumlein. "And since I can't hire anyone who knows how to poach rhinos, I'll have to hire people who can breach a force field."

I frowned. "What are you talking about?"

"Prisoners," he said. "I'll commute the sentence of any prisoner in our jails who can prove to me that he can get through the force field."

"Are you crazy?" I snapped. "You're encouraging them all to become poachers! They're already criminals!"

"It won't be that simple, David," he said calmly. "Any prisoner who accepts my offer must agree to have a tracer chip inserted in his body so we will always know exactly where he is. I think we'll eventually do the same for all the larger animals in the parks, but first comes the anti-poaching squad. We can't hire the expertise that they hired at those ranches in Kenya, but we'll have people who know exactly how poachers breach the force fields, they'll be armed, and we'll be able to trace their movements every minute of the day. It's a start, at least."

"I hope so," I said dubiously.

"I'll tell you something else," Blumlein continued. "We'll catch the poacher, and soon. Given what the horn is worth, only one man on Kilimanjaro will suddenly have that kind of money. If he deposits it here, we'll know instantly. If he deposits it on Earth, I'll ask the banks there to report it. They won't even have to be Kenyan banks; he can't start an account anywhere on Earth without showing them his Kilimanjaro passport."

"I hadn't considered that," I said.

"No reason why you should," he replied. "You're neither a policeman nor a politician."

"We should have him incarcerated in no time."

"You haven't been paying attention to your own arguments," said Blumlein with a laugh. "Whoever he is, we'll reach an accommodation with him, and because of his skills he'll become the leader of our anti-poaching team. Just because we capture *him* doesn't mean collectors will stop offering huge prices for trophies, and that kind of offer always gets a response."

And sure enough, three days later we caught the poacher when he tried to put the money in a safe box under the watchful eye of the bank's security holo camera. Just out of curiosity I went to visit him in his cell. He was a young pastoralist, perhaps sixteen or seventeen years old, named Katoo ole Porola. That sounded familiar, and finally it clicked.

"You're Mawenzi ole Porola's brother!" I said.

He nodded his head unhappily. "There is this girl, Kaelo. I have loved her all my life, and soon I would be able to pay the bride price. But old Simon ole Kipoli's youngest wife died last week, and he has offered to pay the bride price now. She told her father than she will not marry Simon ole Kipoli, that she wants to marry me. But her father grew angry, and threatened to send her back to his brother on Earth for disobeying him. Kaelo and I decided to run away to the city of the *il-makesen,* which is my clan, because women who live in the cities can choose whom they want. But I have no money, and I needed to get some before her father sent her to Earth."

"What gave you the idea of killing the rhino?" I asked.

"My own father speaks of collectors with contempt. I contacted Herbert ole Basinole, whose family moved to the city last year, and he found a collector on Earth. He did this as a friend, and took no money or cattle for his efforts. He just wanted to help Kaelo and me before her father sent her away." He paused, trying to hold back his tears. "I have brought shame on my family, and now I have lost her forever."

"Perhaps not," I said.

He looked at me questioningly.

"Before long someone will come by to speak to you about the future. Unless I miss my guess, you'll be given a chance to redeem yourself. If I were you, I'd agree to their terms."

His face lit up at that.

The next day Herbert ole Basinole received a stern lecture and a tour of the prison from Blumlein himself, and we were assured that there would be no repeat of his efforts as a go-between.

Two weeks later, with a newly-implanted chip, a uniform, a salary, and a title, Katoo ole Parola became Kilimanjaro's first anti-poaching warden. Shortly thereafter the two young lovers were married. Blumlein decreed that no bride price was due, but Katoo insisted that five shillings be taken out of his pay every week for a year and sent to Kaelo's father.

Young Katoo proved to be good at his job. *Too* good. You wouldn't think that a young man performing his job well would bring about the greatest change in our history—but it did.

8 A New Dawn on Kilimanjaro (2241-2243 A.D.)

A year passed without another poaching incident. I considered that a success, and in a way it was. But it also presented us with an unanticipated problem.

When I returned to the office one day after a leisurely lunchtime drive through the nearer of the two game parks, I found a message waiting for me. I activated the computer, and William Blumlein's holo popped into existence.

"Hello, David," he said. "We find ourselves in a bit of a problem here, and I'd very much like your input. I've also invited Joshua. He'll stop by your office after lunch to pick you up and drive you over."

I spent the next twenty minutes trying to figure out what the problem might be. Then Joshua showed up, and we drove to the Council building. An attendant—I hesitate to call him a guard, though he was armed with a laser pistol—was waiting for us, and ushered us into Blumlein's office.

"I'm glad you could both make it," he said. "We have a policy problem that I need to discuss with you."

"Aren't you supposed to discuss them with the Council of Elders?" I asked.

"Eventually I will," he said. "But both of you were involved at the outset of this one, so I want your opinions." He waited until we were seated, and then continued. "I'm sure you know that Katoo ole Porola's anti-poaching squads have been a success."

"I know," I said, frowning. "But how can that be a problem? The alternative was to do nothing and lose our animals to poachers."

"I agree," said Joshua.

"I'd have thought everyone would agree," said Blumlein. "And you know something interesting? We'd both be wrong."

"I don't understand," said Joshua.

"Then let me enlighten you. Now that unscrupulous collectors know there are animals up here, we have to patrol the parks around the clock. That means three shifts per day per park. And to monitor the force field, and place some men inside the parks should anyone get past the outer perimeter, we need at least seven, and preferably eight, men on each shift. Each man requires weapons and various technical devices to spot any breaches in the force field."

He paused and looked at us. "Gentlemen, that's forty salaries and expenses we didn't have a year ago. And since we don't charge the populace for using the parks, they don't bring in a single shilling to help defray expenses. A sizeable minority of the city dwellers feel that we should do away with the parks, turn the land over to the pastoralists who always want more land anyway, and find better uses for the money we have been spending on Katoo's squad."

"I hadn't considered the expenses," I admitted.

"*I* had," said Joshua. "But I had no idea they'd be so high." He frowned. "The Maasai have always lived in harmony with Nature. It's our heritage, and it would be against everything we stand for if we got rid of the parks."

"But you're *not* living in harmony with Nature," Blumlein pointed out gently. "You've enclosed it with a force field."

"Do you *want* to get rid of them, William?" demanded Joshua.

"No, I don't," replied Blumlein. "I just want to point out some of the arguments we'll be facing if we decide to keep them." He turned to me. "Well, historian?"

I shrugged. "We live in a capitalist society. Over the centuries all other economic systems have been failures."

"Go on," said Blumlein, and I could tell he knew what I was about to say and approved of it.

"We're on an artificial, terraformed world," I continued. "We're not going to discover gold or diamonds or fissionable materials on Kilimanjaro. Any wealth we enjoy must be wealth we ourselves create, and that means to continue their existence the parks must become economically self-sufficient. They must pay for Katoo's team, and once they prove they can do that, they will eventually be required to pay for the maintenance of the force field was well. If they can't pay their own way, then they'll have to go."

"I agree completely," said Blumlein. "Now the question is: how can we make the parks pay for themselves?"

"You know the answer," I said.

"Yes, but I'd rather hear it from you," he said with the hint of an amused smile. "That way I won't feel too lonely, getting out ahead of an issue all by myself."

"Hell, you knew it when you called us here," said Joshua irritably. "If we want to keep the parks over the opposition you're receiving, we have to make them self-supporting."

"And that means?" said Blumlein.

"It means opening Kilimanjaro up to tourism from Earth," I said.

"I think you're right, David."

"You *know* I'm right," I said. "You just want me to argue it in front of the Council so the ones who are against it get mad at me instead of you."

Blumlein smiled. "Isn't a politician supposed to protect his ass while he's solving problems?"

"I only know one politician," said Joshua. "And sometimes he annoys the shit out of me."

"Well, he's going to annoy you a lot more," said Blumlein.

"What now?" demanded Joshua.

"Now I want you to think."

"Think about *what*?" replied Joshua, confused.

Blumlein looked at me, and saw that I understood what he was driving at. "Tell him, David," he said.

"It's a game of dominos," I said to Joshua. "Each thing we do leads to another. If we open the game parks to tourists, we're going to need lodges to house them. We're going to need roads from the landing field to the parks. We're going to need *real* game wardens, because if we get enough tourists to pay for the parks, they're inevitably going to do harm to the parks' ecology. We can't let them wander through the parks on foot, not with all the predators we have, so we'll need to import special vehicles, and *that* means we'll need to create roads, or at least tracks, for the vehicles, and we'll need to train some of our people to drive and service those vehicles."

"That's just the tip of the iceberg," added Blumlein, "not that anyone's likely to find any icebergs in Kilimanjaro. We have a landing field that we have named Haven. Right now it's just an empty area. But if we start a tourist industry, we can't have tourists just standing on a field with their baggage until a ship arrives. We'll need a small spaceport, not for the ships—not in the beginning, anyway—but for the tourists. They'll need a place to bring their luggage, to get out of the weather and away from the thrusts of the retro rockets, to eat a meal while waiting for their ships. And we're assuming a daily ship from Earth, the kind that brought the Maasai here to begin with. But the kind of man or woman who can afford the time and expense to come here just to look at animals is probably flying a private ship, so we'll need a hangar, a fueling station, and trained mechanics at the very minimum."

"Then I guess we kill the parks after all," said Joshua.

"Why?" asked Blumlein.

"What you're describing isn't a Maasai Utopia," replied Joshua. "It's closer to a Maasai's idea of hell."

Blumlein turned to me. "Is it, David?"

"It depends on which Maasai you ask," I replied. "Don't forget that back on Earth eighty percent of the Maasai deserted the savannahs for the cities; clearly *they* were interested in profit. And even the pastoralists have never been shy about taking tourists' money. As early as the late 20th century we had model villages that tourists could visit, and wander through, looking into the huts, taking photographs and videos, asking questions, and our *elmoran* spent far more time satisfying the tourists' curiosity then tending their cattle. By the dawn of the 21st century, we had created many jobs related to tourism. Did you know that in the year 2020 A.D. alone, we sold 7,000 authentic Maasai spears? Less than a thousand were sold in Africa; the rest were sold through dealers, or via the internet."

"So was it really hell?" said Blumlein.

"If it wasn't, why did we emigrate to Kilimanjaro?" said Joshua.

"You came here to create a Utopia."

"So did the Kikuyu of Kirinyaga," said Joshua.

"Did they, David?" said Blumlein.

"No," I answered. "They came here to *replace* a Utopia that they thought existed before the coming of the Europeans. We have come here to create one, and we have no blueprint."

"We know what *not* to create," Joshua insisted.

"Do we?" replied Blumlein. "Show me a Maasai who is opposed to wealth, who disdains cattle *and* shillings, and I will agree."

"So will we take money from the hospitals or the farmers to pay for your tourist industry?"

"Wealth isn't finite, Joshua," continued Blumlein. "You can see that yourself, just by observing a herd of cattle. Every time one is born, the herd becomes worth more—and no other herd became worth less because of it. That *creates* wealth. We're examining some of the consequences of creating a park system that pays for itself. It brings in tourist money, money that doesn't exist on Kirinyaga until the tourist spends it. It brings jobs as game wardens, vehicle mechanics, lodge workers—jobs that will not exist until the tourist requires help. The money spent on these jobs will not be taken from someone else on Kirinyaga. It is money that will *increase* our wealth, not merely *redistribute* it."

"Stop lecturing me as if I was a schoolchild!" said Joshua angrily.

"Then stop using a schoolchild's arguments," replied Blumlein. "If the people wanted to live exactly as they lived in Kenya and Tanzania, then they wouldn't have come to Kilimanjaro. Like any potential Utopia, this is an experiment. I'll keep the parks if I can, and I'll deal with what follows as best I can. But if I can't keep the parks, if I can't win a majority of the Elders to my side, I won't quit and return to Earth with my tail between my legs. I'll come up with another blueprint for another Utopia. What I *won't* do is preside over an exact duplicate of life on Earth. If *that* was Utopia, then the Maasai should never have left it in the first place."

"It was closer than what you're proposing," insisted Joshua.

"You'll have to forgive me if I disagree with you," said Blumlein.

"You can disagree with me in front of the Council," said Joshua, "because that's where I intend to make my arguments."

"That's the best place for them," agreed Blumlein. "I'll see you there."

Joshua walked to the door, then turned to me. "Are you coming, David?" he said, still agitated.

"I have some further business to discuss with David," said Blumlein. "I'll see that he's provided a ride when we're finished."

Joshua left without another word. Blumlein waited a moment to make sure he wasn't coming back, then turned to me. "Thank you for not mentioning it, David," he said.

"I'm surprised he didn't think of it himself," I replied. "It was obvious."

"Only to an historian," said Blumlein. "Remember, Africa hasn't had any large mammals for a couple of centuries, and they did everything they could to protect them for the half century before that. How could he know about culling?"

"Still," I said, "he should have been able to figure out that one rhino horn, not poached but sacrificed, could support the two parks for twenty years. Long enough to grow a few more rhinos, and sacrifice another."

"I can't argue with the math," agreed Blumlein.

"What will you do if he thinks of it in time to mention it to the Council?" I asked.

"The math is indisputable, but I can argue with the morality. The game parks culled animals when they exceeded the parks' capacity to feed them. It was a quick death in lieu of death by slow starvation. More to the point, the animals were there first, and were required to make an accommodation with the human inhabitants. Whereas absolutely nothing was here. This is an artificial world with no native life forms. We have rhinos and other animals because we wanted them, we cloned them, and we nurtured them, and it is immoral to kill even one of them as a matter of economic convenience."

"I was right," I said.

"About what?"

"This job," I said. "You're the right man for it."

"I've barely had time to get my feet wet," replied Blumlein. "The really interesting part lies ahead."

Then he got busy with the really interesting part.

He made his case before the Council, and made it well. It was the first time Joshua ole Saibull had ever lost a unanimous decision.

Within a month construction began on two luxury lodges, one in each park, run by Maasai in crisp green uniforms. Biologists were invited from Earth to lecture the new staff on the intricacies of their jobs and the ecosystems. Engineers came to teach our new mechanics how to keep the lodges' systems functioning. Experts were imported to train our new chefs, waiters and concierges.

Outside each park were a pair of brand-new *manyattas*. Articulate young men and women, who discarded their shorts and shirts each morning in favor of their red robes, took visitors on a tour of the *manyattas*, relating fact, history and legend with equal enthusiasm.

Within a year we had built a spaceport, with room for expansion. Some of our men and women were sent to Earth to learn the major tourist languages, others to study the workings of more complex spaceports against the day that ours, too, became busier and more complex.

The spaceport originally housed a currency exchange, but this soon became a full service bank. In fact, small banks were starting to spring up across the savannah so that the pastoralists would not have to bring the money they made from tourists all the way into the cities.

The attractions we offered increased. Weddings were open to the (paying) public. So was the Eunoto ceremony. The traditional Maasai dances, in which the *elmoran* jump straight up and down endlessly, proved to be an unsatisfactory attraction, so we hired choreographers from the Shona and Xhosa tribes to enliven them.

One very fair-skinned tourist received a serious sunburn, and who should treat him but the former *laiboni*-turned-nurse Sokoine ole Parasayip? Not only that, but once the tourist found out that he'd been nursed by a genuine witch doctor, he insisted on taking home some of the generic ointment Sokoine had used on him. This was not lost on Sokoine or his superiors, and within a month *Authentic Laiboni Skin Care* was being packaged here and exported not only to Earth but to the other Eutopian colonies as well.

It was an exciting time to be on Kilimanjaro, to see the many changes that were occurring in our society. Every day brought a new innovation. The few that didn't work were replaced by those that did.

It was almost two years to the day after Joshua had stormed out of the office that I found myself sitting on the shaded patio of Blumlein's new house, sharing a drink with him.

"You should be very proud of yourself," I told him. "You seem to have the golden touch. Everything's running like clockwork."

"Come on, David," he said. "You're an historian. You know better."

I stared at his questioningly.

"We've already got our first measurable air pollution," said Blumlein. "Sooner or later some new virus is going to strike the game parks, and if it hits the predators we'll have to cull the larger herbivores or they'll eat themselves out of the park, and if it hits the herbivores will have to cull the predators or they'll die of slow starvation. With all the money floating around the savannah, it's going to be impossible for the traditionalists to continue to use their cattle as currency. We're undergoing a nine percent inflation rate right now, and even after we cure that, no economy ever goes too long without a recession. Other Eutopian worlds have noticed what we've done, and a few are following suit; eventually we'll have to battle them for tourist shillings."

"So you don't think it will last?"

"Nothing lasts, David," he replied easily. "The only question is whether it will outlast us."

"That makes it sound very much like you think our Utopia is a failure."

He took a sip of his drink. "You're looking at it all wrong. Everyone has pitched in, planning and working, for the past two years. That's the key, and that's where Kirinyaga made its error."

I frowned. "I'm not sure what you're getting at."

"Men have always thrived on challenges," he said with the hint of a smile. "Has it ever occurred to you, David, that perhaps Utopia isn't an end result at all, but rather the simple act of striving for that result?"

It hadn't.

But I've thought a lot about it since that night, and I think maybe he was right.

At least I don't worry about the future anymore.